ETHEL WILSON was born in Port Elizabeth, South Africa, in 1888. She was taken to England at the age of two after her mother died. Seven years later her father died, and in 1898 she came to Vancouver to live with her maternal grandmother. She received her teacher's certificate from the Vancouver Normal School in 1907 and taught in many local elementary schools until her marriage in 1921.

In the 1930s Wilson published a few short stories and began a series of family reminiscences which were later transformed into *The Innocent Traveller*. Her first published novel, *Hetty Dorval*, appeared in 1947, and her fiction career ended fourteen years later with the publication of her story collection, *Mrs. Golightly and Other Stories*. Through her compassionate and often ironic narration, Wilson explores in her fiction the moral lives of her characters.

For her contribution to Canadian literature, Wilson was awarded the Canada Council Medal in 1961 and the Lorne Pierce Medal of the Royal Society of Canada in 1964. Her husband died in 1966, and she spent her later years in seclusion and ill-health.

Ethel Wilson died in Vancouver in 1980.

THE NEW CANADIAN LIBRARY

General Editor: David Staines

ADVISORY BOARD
Alice Munro
W.H. New
Guy Vanderhaeghe

ETHEL WILSON

Love and Salt Water

With an Afterword by Anne Marriott

Copyright © 1990 by University of British Columbia Library,
by arrangement with Macmillan of Canada
Afterword copyright © 1990 by Anne Marriott

This book was first published in 1956 by The Macmillan
Company of Canada Limited.

Reprinted 1990

All rights reserved. The use of any part of this publication
reproduced, transmitted in any form or by any means,
electronic, mechanical, photocopying, recording, or
otherwise, or stored in a retrieval system, without the prior
written consent of the publisher – or, in the case of
photocopying or other reprography copying, a licence from
Canadian Reprography Collective – is an infringement of the
copyright law.

Canadian Cataloguing in Publication Data

Wilson, Ethel, 1888-1980
Love and Salt Water

(New Canadian library)
Includes bibliographical references.
ISBN 0-7710-8957-0

I. Title. II. Series.

PS8545.I62L6 1990   C813'.54   C90-093966-4
PR9199.3.W5L6 1990

Printed and bound in Canada

Published by arrangement with Macmillan of Canada

McClelland & Stewart Inc.
The Canadian Publishers
481 University Avenue
Toronto, Ontario
M5G 2E9

*This tale is affectionately inscribed
to my uncle,* W.H.M.,
*who was young Skookoonia-goose
(North West Territories 1884)
and to* W.M.B., N.D.F., G.L.E.
*who – with courage, selflessness,
good sense and good humour – build*

Contents

PART ONE	A Voyage	9
PART TWO	A Few Years	61
PART THREE	A Scar	101

Afterword 173

PART ONE

A Voyage

One

WHEN ELLEN CUPPY was eleven years old and sat on the foot of the bed, getting in the way of her big sister Nora who was packing her suitcases with great care, she thought how sad it was for Nora, who was so fair and pretty, to marry that old Mr. Morgan Peake who was all of forty; yet Nora did not seem to mind, but shook out the crêpe de Chine nightdresses and laid them on the bed and slowly folded them again with tissue paper in between, and Ellen thought that Nora was like a lamb getting ready for the sacrifice; and thinking of lambs and sacrifices she thought of garlands and timbrels and damsels and maidens and vestal virgins, such things as she read about and liked the sound of but did not understand.

She said, rocking as she sat, "Nora, what is a virgin?", but Nora gently shook out the silken garment again and did not listen.

"Listen, Nora, what *is* a virgin anyway?"

"A virgin?" said Nora distrait. "Oh, it's a biblical character."

"I know that. But what *is* it? Are you a virgin, Nora?"

"Me?" said Nora, looking up. "Certainly not! Well, perhaps, in a way. Will you sit still, or get off the bed . . . I can't fold with you jiggling."

"Mother," said Ellen to her mother who came into the bedroom, "what is a virgin? What do they do?"

"It's a young girl," said her mother. "Give me that nightdress, dear, I'll fold it . . . they don't do anything that I know of . . . you should have put the dress in first . . . "

"You mean they just stick around? What good are they? What are they for?"

"Oh," said her mother, straightening up, "will you ever be quiet just for a minute, Gypsy! Don't bother Nora now; get off the bed, Nora needs the space . . . you little mosquito . . . time for you to go to bed", and she took Ellen by the shoulders and ran her out of the room and into her own bedroom. "Good night, pet, and don't forget to brush your teeth," she said, and went back to the bride.

"My goodness," said Ellen, sauntering about her bedroom and practising fancy steps, "I'd hate to be Nora! I don't call that a love affair, marrying that old Mr. Peake", and she stopped her dance steps and took out from amongst her books an adventure story called *Wallaby Will* and went to bed and forgot about Nora and also about being a bridesmaid the next day.

Two

LARGE DEEP-SEA freighters which are also passenger boats steam into Vancouver harbour. Some of the freighters can accommodate about twelve passengers. Some take fifty or even sixty. They come through the Panama Canal, from across the Pacific Ocean, and beyond.

Long before Nora was married, Mrs. Cuppy used to take the children into the Park. They would watch from the shore, looking westward, a gliding freighter which had just shown its bow around the distant southern point of land. For some time the freighter seemed to ride balanced on the line of the horizon.

"You could push it off with your finger," said Ellen.

"Don't be silly. You couldn't," said Nora, although she was ten years older.

The freighter, moving slowly along the dividing line of sea and sky as along a tight-rope, gradually turned toward Vancouver and changed its appearance to an amazing degree. The ship which had appeared excessively long and elegant became foreshortened, and was transformed to a large squat black object approaching upon the ocean. It became a different ship. The ship passed Bowen Island, passed the lighthouse, and, travelling with admirable slowness and intelligence, reassumed in front of their eyes its appearance of length and slimness, passed in front of the mountains, disappeared behind the wooded point of the Park, and entered the harbour which is part of the inlet which Captain George Vancouver named Burrard Inlet. The children could not see the freighter now, the high forests of the Park intervened, but they could picture it steaming slowly through the Narrows, proceeding up Burrard Inlet, coming into the docks or, perhaps, anchoring in the stream for the time being.

Sometimes Nora and Ellen and their mother walked or drove in the Park, and on the inner side – that is, the side of the Park which looks upon the busy harbour, not upon the open sea – they stood, or sat on the grass, and watched the freighters (looking bigger than usual) pass quite close to them and vanish under the Lions' Gate Bridge and through the Narrows, out to sea. Sometimes the big ships rode high in the water but often they were laden and lay low and handsome. The pleasure of watching the deep-sea freighters in the inner harbour was enhanced by the multiplicity of smaller ships which peppered the water, tugs travelling slowly with their tows or tearing out alone through the Narrows with the racing tide, seiners, and gillnetters, tankers, coasting vessels; but the tugs and the freighters gave most life to the scene. There were also multitudes of sea-birds and particularly the cormorants.

It was not perhaps strange that the freighters were important to Mother and to Ellen. They were not so important to Nora, whose childhood did not seem to last very long as she was practical by early nature and married young; her dreamy fairness was delusive; she did not really care for gazing at birds and boats. Mother's bedroom window looked to the south over False Creek and to the west over the open sea, and for as long as Ellen could remember she had knelt on the windowseat, and had called out "Mother, there's a freighter!" and her mother had come to look, or Mother had called "Look, Gypsy, there's a freighter!" It seems ridiculous that ordinary ships moving upon the water should exercise a never-dying interest, but so it was with Mother and Ellen, and Mother often said "Some day, when Father has time, Gypsy, we'll go on a freighter", and Ellen believed her.

Ellen and her mother lived very much in each other's society, because when Ellen was little, Nora had begun to be big, and then, when Nora was not yet twenty-one, to everyone's surprise she married Mr. Morgan Peake, who was a well-known lawyer and also a Member of Parliament. He was dark and square with jutting eyebrows and was fully nineteen years older than his bride. He was not even a widower and Nora was his first real love, not counting two long-past episodes before he became ambitious. Ambition developed in him fairly early but he was not its slave. As a husband he was admirable, but his devotion to Nora had the effect of spoiling her. She was reasonably fond of him, and, as she did not know the force of passion, she retained her unflawed good looks, and the train of her life in which she sat as a beautiful passenger was drawn as it were by a diesel engine which made travelling too smooth. She became very "smart", and her smartness had a casual or beguiling quality of indifference.

Nora was placidly fond of her mother, and of her father too; but as her father was seldom at home and she was used to her mother, and as she had little imagination, her love for her father and mother made few demands upon her. She was not ardent.

Since Mr. Cuppy was usually in Mexico or Persia or New York or in such nextdoor places as Alberta or Northern Saskatchewan – anywhere where the presence of oil was suspected or decisions about oil could be made – the result was that although he and his wife loved each other dearly, he was an absentee husband. That being the case, Mrs. Cuppy had spent barely one-third of their married life with him. One result of this was that she and their little daughter Gypsy were indispensable to each other. Fortunately Gypsy had many school friends too. Her chief friends were Isa Graham and Billy Peake, who was the eldest of the three sons of Mr. and Mrs. Dick Peake who were relatives of Morgan, Nora's husband. At first, Mrs. Cuppy was not pleased about Nora's marriage, and neither was her husband. They thought Morgan was far too old for Nora – and so he was – and that she could not really love him. Therefore was the marriage wise and safe? It was no good worrying, because, although Nora did not seem to know what love was in Mrs. Cuppy's sense of the word "love", her mind was set to Morgan and she was gently obstinate. She seemed happy, and as Morgan's young wife she was very successful. Much of her time was spent in Ottawa when the House was sitting. Father was away; Nora was away; and fortunately Ellen and her mother were the best of companions. Never was there a luckier girl than Ellen Cuppy with such a merry dear mother.

When Mr. and Mrs. Cuppy were first married, Frank Cuppy intended to take his wife always with him on these journeys as soon as they could afford it. But before they could afford it Nora was born, and when they could afford it Susan Cuppy was occupied with looking after their two girls. She put away, as well as she could, the regrets that were sometimes uppermost that she had been deprived of going with her husband to strange and distant places. She would have liked to see these uncomfortable places. She would have liked to meet the men of all kinds, foreign and domestic, distinguished and ordinary, that her husband met in these places, and sometimes the women too; and she would like to have surveyed those peculiar scenes. Frank was not interested in women as women; he much preferred the company of men; but his wife did not take her immunity from trouble entirely for granted, as Frank was too good-looking. When he came home it was nearly his greatest pleasure in life to be with his wife Susan and his tall fair daughter and his little dark daughter. Perhaps it was his greatest pleasure. He did not care for society at large and was apt to become glum in the presence of people in whom he was not interested. When he was glum he was strikingly handsome but forbidding. Although his wife was for these reasons somewhat deprived of the society of men (which she very much enjoyed), and of women, she said to herself that you can't have things both ways and thank goodness I have Gypsy, and Frank cares most for me and for the children – and, of course, for finding oil. He did not at first really care about money. When, on his returns home, he almost immediately departed again, she did her best to be philosophical.

As Frank Cuppy became rich or, at least, comfortable, he

suggested to his wife that she should move into a new part of Vancouver, but she said No. She said that she preferred to stay beside False Creek and English Bay for otherwise she would miss the view of the ocean from the windows, and the nearness to the Park where she could drive and walk so easily. At the weekends Gypsy went with her unless she stayed with Isa Graham as she often did. When Frank went away again he was not quite content about his wife Susan. He bought her a nice new roadster which emancipated her a good deal, and he often sent strange and beautiful presents to her and to the girls and then felt easier in his mind. He could not say when this section of his life would end. He put away the thought of it because he honestly knew that it would never end but would become more and more continuous and exacting and successful. When Gypsy grew a little older and went – perhaps – to a university, Susan would at last come with him sometimes; and so we confidently plan our lives.

"Some day, darling," said Susan, looking up at him as they stood watching a great white ship glide below the Lions' Gate Bridge and vanish – their vision blocked by forest – out to sea, "some day we'll all go off on a freighter together – anywhere – anywhere . . . you and Gypsy and me . . . "

"We will," said her husband (when?).

"Promise, Daddy! Promise!" said Ellen.

"Promise," said her father.

When these three went walking in the Park together they were better to look at than most people. Mrs. Cuppy was small and slim and tossed herself gaily along as she walked with her husband. She was completely happy. Frank Cuppy was tall, erect, and spare. Ellen was a leggy child with a small good head and bright dark eyes. They walked well. No wonder people liked to look at them. There should be many more people to look at like Mr. and Mrs. Cuppy and their daughter Ellen walking so well together, what with modern advantages, and if Nora had been walking with them in her tall fair beauty they would have looked finer still. Morgan would have pulled the average of looks down, but not if his mind and judgment could have been made visible. Morgan and Nora did not enjoy walking in parks. Morgan was only a few years younger than Frank Cuppy but in his weighty oracular way he was as old. The two men were companionable on the rare occasions when they saw each other, talking as two men and not as father-in-law and son-in-law, but Frank Cuppy at first felt the situation to be a little silly.

Susan knew that as they walked, and as she and Gypsy talked, Frank did not always hear what they said, although his hearing was perfect. He habitually thought of other things, she was sure, but she could not alter that and, as she loved him and he loved her, she did not mind much. She was right. As Frank walked with Susan and Gypsy he was continuing his disagreement in opinion with Dr. Antonio Mattaneo whom he neither liked nor trusted, and he was summoning a further argument. The sound of his wife and daughter talking was a pleasant accompaniment as long as he was not required to listen and answer, which it never occurred to him to do. Men are driven to this in self-defence.

"Listen! Listen! Answer me at once! You're not even *listening!*" said Ellen, dancing round in front of him and walking backwards. "What kind of a father are you that doesn't even listen to his own daughter!" and Frank came back from where he had been glowering at Dr. Mattaneo with whom he continued to disagree.

Next day Father had to return unexpectedly to Mexico and so Nora, arriving from Ottawa, missed him after all.

"If I'd only known, I'd have flown on Tuesday," she said.

"But he didn't know," said Mother.

"He never does, poor Marmee," said Nora, smiling gently at her mother.

"He can't help it!" said Mother, defending.

"I know."

Three

ON ELLEN'S sixteenth birthday her mother gave her a party. The party consisted of Mr. and Mrs. Graham and Isa and her brother and sister, and Mr. and Mrs. Dick Peake (she was Aunt Maury Peake) and their three boys and Mother and Ellen. Morgan was in Ottawa, and Nora at this late date had begun to be pregnant, and was uncomfortable, so neither of them was able to be at the party.

Mother had planned a garden supper early. Then they would all go to the Theatre under the Stars to a beautiful musical show. But when the day came, Mother did not feel well and had, unwillingly, to forgo the supper part of the party, and then she decided not to go to the Theatre under the Stars, but to have a good rest, and Mr. Dick Peake and Mr. Graham would take care of them all.

Ellen was surprised as her mother was always well, and she was a little disturbed. "Let me stay at home," she said, looking up the staircase at her mother with bright dark eyes.

Her mother, looking down on her daughter, laughed and said, "It musta been something I ett. It's nothing, nothing, Gypsy. You go along, and if my light's on when you come home, come in and tell me all about it. But if my light's off you'll know I'm asleep and tell me tomorrow. Take the key."

"All right, Mother," said Ellen, reluctant to leave her, but eager to go.

"Have a good time, pet," said her mother. She turned to go

up the stairs, and those were the last words Ellen ever heard her mother say.

When they came home the house was dark. "The house is dark!" they said.

"She's asleep," said Ellen, and Billy Peake went with her to the front door. Ellen looked at the black front of the house with only the street lights reflected from the black windows and knew that her mother must have fallen asleep soon, before there was a need for lights in the hall. They quietly put the key in the lock and then she went into the house and felt deprived because she was not going into Mother's room to sit on her bed and tell her all about the play and how funny it was and what Mr. Graham said, particularly as it was Mother's party; but she would have to put it off until morning.

Next morning Ellen woke late. She lay looking at the ceiling for a while and her eyes crinkled in laughter as she thought of what Mr. Graham said, and then she jumped up and ran in her nightdress to her mother's room. It was still dark, or at least the light of morning came round the edges of the blinds. Ellen went in cautiously as her mother seemed to be asleep. She would not wake her, but if her mother woke now, at this minute, Ellen could kiss her and find out how she was feeling, and then she would go downstairs in her dressing-gown and make them both some breakfast and bring it upstairs and tell her about the play.

Ellen went barefoot to the side of the bed and bent to look at her mother who lay still. Ellen's eyes were now accustomed to the half-light, and she saw that on Mother's face was a strange look of surprise. "Mother," she said, bending nearer. Then, louder, "Mother!"

Her mother did not change or answer.

Ellen, standing there – Ellen, who had been very happy, began to tremble. Her hands crept slowly to her face and she continued looking at her mother's face which was not as her mother's face. She forced herself to speak again, louder.

"Mother." But her mother lay still.

Ellen dared not leave the bedside and draw the blinds, but

stood there in the stillness. The glow of full day lighted the room round the edges of the blinds. At last she knelt down and touched the curve of her mother's body and moved her hand along the rigid bend of her leg. She did not at first dare to touch her face. Or her hand. At last she touched her mother's hand, and then touched gently the surprised face. This must be true although it can't be true. The impossible and the incredible invaded everything in the girl's world. Is this what it is? Where's Father? Oh, what shall I do, Mother? And she gave a little cry and got up from her knees and drew back from the bed and continued looking at her dear mother.

If I do nothing, she thought wildly and childishly, Mother can't possibly be dead. It's if I tell people, then that makes it true, one person telling another person – and she saw the train of words and talk and tears and telephonings and telegrams and arrangements confusedly in a whirling cloud; and yet she could not foresee the smallest part of these arrangements and decisions because she was so young (sixteen years old yesterday) and ignorant.

She stretched out her hand toward her mother's telephone and drew it back, to defend her mother and herself – and her father too – just for a few more moments, against her mother having died. Yet she was sure her mother had died. This must be what that is.

When she had cried awhile, standing there in her nightdress in the stillness of the room, very frightened with this quiet stranger her dear mother, she managed to pick up the telephone because she must at some time pick it up, and all the while she never took her eyes off her mother whom she was now giving over to other people's talk and arrangements (it was strange how strongly Ellen felt this as the minutes advanced). Poor Nora, she thought, and this thought extended beyond herself and her mother, to Nora. Poor Nora, what will happen to her like she is now if I tell her this, I don't know, I don't know about these things, and she looked round the room, poor child. I will tell Aunt Maury, and soon Aunt Maury Peake heard Ellen weeping some words over the telephone.

Ellen knew that, with her first weeping to Aunt Maury on the telephone, their life together, Mother and Gypsy, was over for ever, was ended, and arrangements had begun.

Death and arrangements. And only one hour ago she did not know this, and one night ago her mother was here, and now arrangements were beginning.

Before Ellen, weeping, telephoned Aunt Maury Peake, she knew that this had always been ordained and that Mother's death was already established; as it were a long time ago.

Four

"AT LEAST, it's the best solution," said Morgan to his newspaper.

"There is no solution," said his wife.

Morgan turned the page of the newspaper. He said (for the twentieth time, he thought), sensibly and kindly, "Yes, there is a solution. When you are faced with a situation, you make your choice, dolling. This is the best solution."

"At least it will not keep her out of school for more than a month."

"It is more important than school just now," said Morgan.

"It will provide a necessary break for her, and then she will settle in more contentedly wherever she is," said Nora, "and it will be good for Father to have her with him." Nora had said all this many times, because the arrangements for the funeral, and the decisions about the house and the furniture, and the decisions about Gypsy, and the decision that she should accompany her father on a voyage, and his decision that since he had to go to Teheran after Christmas he would have the previous month with Gypsy and they could spend Christmas at sea ("it will be much easier for them to have Christmas at sea, nothing could be better," said everybody round and round) – all these arrangements in which Ellen had become some sort of pawn had been discussed in the family and with close friends, knee to knee and over the telephone, and decisions had been made. Nora had talked to Aunt Maury, and to Morgan's sisters-in-law, and to a Miss Sneddon, and to Isa's mother, and each of these had discussed with each other, and with others. She had also talked daily to Morgan, and this was odd because she was not by nature a talker. But arrangements were so various: "the trunks can be kept in our basement but we have not room for the furniture", "they had better be stored", "I do not approve of black", "these people have not such good references. I myself would not fancy them as tenants", "she can board at the school, it would be more lively", "she should stay at Nora's", "Maury Peake would take her but with all those boys . . . ", "I heard she was going to Isa Graham's", "it will be a good solution, their going on this trip", "it will be a good solution", and all this to-do and arrangement was occasioned by the innocent death of Gypsy's mother. Things had been better as they were.

Morgan, on whom talk fell daily, would have liked to say that conversation too often repeated becomes redundant and tedious, but his wife looked frail.

"They will be about four weeks in reaching London, Father says, not three," said Nora fingering a letter, "and then Gypsy can fly back here. I think she'd better go to . . . "

"The P.M. has a chill," said Morgan. "Would you like this piece of the paper, dolling?"

"Because *then*," continued Nora, "May Cross opens on the fifteenth and she can still come back for the weekends. I think she looks listless."

"Well," said Morgan, defeated, "it was a great shock." He meant this, but had said it too often.

"Yes, a *very* great shock," said Nora.

Ellen came into the room and the conversation was changed.

Five

BECAUSE FRANK CUPPY had always been too busy and had worked under pressure he had never stopped to consider and therefore had never known the fact that bereavement with regret is the worst and irrevocable ill that can befall a man. Except in the matter of deadlines ("plane leaves 4.30 a.m.") he was not one of those who hear Time's winged chariot, and now here was Time made visible. Finality was made visible and tangible. Susan had been his wife for twenty-seven years, and suddenly she had gone irrevocably with those years into some abyss of memory.

It is a good solution, he said drearily to himself, taking Gypsy on this trip, she needs it, I need her – and in Susan's absence which made the voyage so poignant, he felt that he was fulfilling what Susan would wish. "Yes, Frank," he could hear her saying in her light earnest way, "under these conditions I think it is the best solution."

"I hope none of these blasted people will come down to the freighter to see us off," he growled. But the blasted people of all ages who were close friends of the Cuppy family and of the Morgan Peakes discussed among themselves, and some said, "It would be awful their going away with no one down to see them off, just like a funeral all over again. We've decided to go." Others said, "You don't know Frank Cuppy. He'll curse us for going down. He'll want to slip off quietly and naturally with Gypsy and no fuss. We've decided not to go."

The result was that about forty people came to see them

off; flowers evoking recent memory were in Ellen's little cabin; some friends sped away, and some stayed conversing; everyone felt a muted exuberance in spite of themselves; there were presents; the young people did not think it suitable to say "Well, have a good time" and they did not know what else you say last thing when people go away on a trip, until someone remembered "So long, mind you write", which was non-committal and took on generally. Frank Cuppy gave everybody Hollands gin in the lounge because people felt that was what you should drink on a Dutch ship, and the girls and boys who came to see Gypsy off drank a nasty sweet syrup. Father and daughter were grateful, and glad to see the last wellwisher go, and the wellwishers left and continued in their cars to contemplate the pathos of Frank and Ellen going off like this but thought it was the best solution.

Ellen and her father in an unspoken revulsion of feeling walked and walked round the deck before going in to unpack; unknown revellers – as the evening grew late – sang songs on the dockside and laughed and called, serenading like cats either the captain, some passengers, or the crew, or just on account of Hollands gin and a feeling for music. They were repetitive and it was nice to leave them and put to sea in the fine fresh night air.

When Ellen's baggage was unpacked and her cabin looked neat and pleasant with the bright faces of the flowers, she undressed and then her father came in to kiss her good-night and as he did that Ellen began to cry.

Frank sat down beside her on the bunk and very awkwardly and with great difficulty said what he had to say. Holding her hands in a manner quite unlike himself but as he might once have done at some time with Susan, he told Ellen that Mother would want them to do this, and she would want them to be as happy as they could. Nothing ever could alter – well, he did not know what to say. But nothing ever could alter what had happened to them and what they felt about it. Ellen *must* remember, and he pressed her hands, that Mother would be sorry if they were not happy, because Mother was secure in their minds (he meant in their hearts, but he could not say that). So it was no kindness or reverence to Mother not to allow happiness because she would know how it was and that they would never for a moment forget.

Ellen got off the bunk where she was curled up and said "I'll try", and she had the first faint feeling of unfairness to Father that she showed her sorrow so plainly. It would be better tomorrow.

As she kissed her father good-night the tears welled again, but he smacked her bottom and then they both felt better. Leaving, he turned to say, "Did you remember your pills? The ship's rolling a bit and it can be rough down this piece of coast."

As Frank went back to his cabin next door the unaccustomed domesticity of telling his daughter to take her pills lifted his spirits, which needed lifting. Life was a stale ditch.

Next day the ship began its insidious assuagement. Frank and Ellen walked round and round the deck ("Walk her, Frank," Maury had said, "it's good medicine. The ship will do the rest"), and the wind whipped them and rain stung their faces and the great grey waves came slowly toward the ship from as far west as one could see till mist closed down. Then the steward came with hot soup. It was astonishing how well they felt and how feelings shook into place. Then, in spite of the lurching ship, they played shuffle-board on a covered deck until they went down to lunch.

Six

GYPSY TO Nora. Mailed in San Francisco.

Dear Nolly,
How are you. Feeling better I hope. You were awfully good and I was sorry you had all that rush. There were hoards of people to see us off, Isa will tell you. I had ten boxes of flowers. Our cabins are lovely and mine is very small but nice. Everybody is Dutch I mean the officers and the crew. We have not seen them much yet. Father is feeling better I think and we walked miles. Will you ask Isa to go and look in the small trunk in your basement and get out my red shirt and send it air mail to Los Angeles. We shall stay here loading things for days and days the way we are going. We are at the first officer's table only he is never there and we shall get as fat as pigs. The other people will come on board at San Francisco. There is just a Major Raymond Clark at our table who is nice but a very nosey man. He is what you would call a young old man or an old young man I think the latter. He talks too much for my taste and is a funny-man. However Father says we might be much worse off as he is a good fellow. He seems to know about Father. He tries to call me Gypsy but I shall not allow it. Those pills were wonderful, I hadn't a quam although it was quite rough

on the way down. I love the ship in spite of you know. I hope some younger people come on board. Everyone is 80. There is even a woman in a wheel chair. You wonder why such people come. How is Morgan. Father and I send our love and don't forget the shirt will you.

With love Gypsy.

Seven

G YPSY TO Billy Peake. Mailed in Los Angeles.

Dear William
This is a lovely pen. You couldn't have given me anything I like better. I wish it could spell that would be a real help. You know me! Imagine its 9 days since we left and that is a whole voyage in itself. It is very interesting watching the stevedores loading the ship with all kinds of things from motorcars to sacks of Borax. What on earth do people do with all that Borax. I never saw anyone as slow as these stevedores both black and white and so much standing about but when they actually get going with little trucks and machinery and things they just put their fingers on the right spot and everything falls into place so I suppose they know their jobs. San Francisco is lovely and Los Angeles was huge. It was exciting to feel you were in Hollywood but we didn't even see a single star. So far everyone on the ship except the officers and crew are about 70. I am hoping someone young will come on the ship at the last moment here. It is awful to be the only young person and I wish I could go down to the sailors who are all young and sing away like anything and wear a pair of

jeans and help scrape and paint and scrub. However I am with Father and that was the idea, and it is wonderful. I will try to find that optical illusion set in London but of course I don't know where to go yet. Don't forget me now Billy or I won't look for the set. Give Uncle Dick and Aunt Maury my love.
Yours ITBOF.

                                                      Gypsy.

    Thanks again for the pen.

Eight

GYPSY TO Isa Graham. Mailed at Panama City.

Dear Isa, my golly all the thank you letters I've written. I told you on my p.c. that I'd wait to write you a real letter. On this ship Isa life begins at 60 or maybe 40 at least. If it weren't for being with Father and why we came I'd go out of my mind, and there are all those young sailors and even a young boy sailor about 13 I should think he's the bosun's grandson and almost too pretty for a boy, and here's me with all these old people drinking Old Fashions and gin all the time they don't even get drunk but what they can find to talk about all the time. They talk and talk.

A nice thing has happened, the swimming pool is up and I swim and dry out nearly all day long and now they dance at night on deck you should see them. There is a Major Clark at our table that I didn't like at first he is too smart aleck and tried to call me Gypsy and when I said my name was Ellen he pretended to go stuffy about it and calls me Miss Cuppy and nothing else but. It sounds funny. He is very keen on Christian names a lot of these old people are but what I do like about him now he is a beautiful dancer and we dance most of the evening every evening and he has taught me a lot of steps. Imagine, he's bald and the youngest kind of person there is except Father and Father doesn't like dancing. Oh there's so much to tell you! We have already seen heaps of dolphins or porpoises they say, and some flying fish it is lovely, so even if you're bored with nobody young except the sailors there's a lot that's lovely and the ship going on and on and on. Father seems relaxed to me and better. I will tell you about the people at our table and then it will be lunch. How we do eat. Now I have to stop.

Next day.

About the table. The first officer is middle age and very polite but not often there. At San Francisco there was a Mr. and Mrs. Bird and a Mrs. Gracey came on and that makes six of us without the 1st officer. Mr. and Mrs. Bird are all right and she talks non stop and Mrs. Gracey is a quiet person and a bit younger. This Major Clark has got the feeling that things aren't going well unless everybody calls Christian names or fancy names and I simply can't say Raymond and so of course I am Miss Cuppy. He is really very cheeky. Besides naming Mrs. Bird Lady Bird and then Mr. Bird Lord Bird, we hadn't been out of San Francisco two days before he began calling Mrs. Gracey Velvet Eyes and Plush Eyes and Pansy Eyes because she has really lovely solid brown eyes, and she also has fair hair I think its real. Otherwise you wouldn't notice her much as she dresses plainly and is quiet. She might be tired. She doesn't let on that Major C. registers at all and I think that's a good idea. But what I was going to tell you was about the coincidence. I was surprised but Father says they often happen on board ship. This Major C. took the passenger list and he read Mr. François Cuppy and he said was Father French and had that been François Coupé. And Father said no, it was a place and said about his being born up at François Lake in Northern B.C. when there was not a human being for miles and then Mrs. Gracey got quite excited. She said that Mrs. N. Gracey was Mrs. Nicola Gracey, and her father lived all his boyhood in a place called Nicola Valley in the interior of B.C. with an old settler uncle who drove cattle in from the States in the sixties. And she said her father came back to California when he was a young boy and when he married he called his daughter Nicola because it was a pretty name and he liked the place. And then they all told coincidences. But believe me, with that Major C. by the time we got to Los Angeles it was Raymond (but not me!) and Lord Bird and Lady Bird and Nicola and Miss Cuppy and Father called France. The whole table calls him France now. I don't like it and I don't know whether he does. It makes him sound like a different person.

Father and Major C. and Mrs. Gracey and I do nearly everything together and every day we swim and play shuffleboard and we play bridge and Lord and Lady Bird cut in. They say we are going to be held up either at Panama City or Colon with a strike and it all makes the voyage much longer. The weather is lovely and hot and you should see the turtles swimming in the water but I love the dolphins the porpoises best. The night before Christmas the bosun has invited us four to go to hear the seamen's Christmas singing. The Chief Steward will take us. I could tell you heaps more but must stop now. I can't tell you how queer it is when we stop to think and suddenly I think can this be Father and me and all this and I get awfully upset Isa but what can you do. But believe me Isa I don't for one minute forget.

With love Gypsy.

Oh, I got the shirt. Thank you. Give my love to your Mother.

Nine

THE FREIGHTER balances on the horizon line, turns, and approaches its destination. It is merely a ship, and people going about their business see idly and equally and nearer at hand that Coca-Cola refreshes and that bigger and better cars are on their way and these things obscure the ship. But watchers on the shore or at windows feel afresh the kindling interest of the long in-coming or out-going deep-sea freighter, and something in the mind says I will go some day, somewhere, anywhere.

In the freighter are several worlds, invisible to the watcher. The Captain and his Senior and Junior Officers have one world to which is annexed the world below deck which is a world of old experienced hands and muscular slow-moving quick-leaping young men, admirable to see. There is the world of passengers, who assemble at port after port until the complement is full, the dining-saloon tables are filled, and the passengers, looking around them, begin to recognize faces and smile pleasantly or avoid their neighbours, according to their dispositions. Passengers on deep-sea freighters are different from other passengers. They travel on a deep-sea freighter either because at last they have saved up enough for the voyage which they have so long anticipated (this is the voyage of a lifetime); or because they are fatigued with the pressures of their lives and the voyage will prove some kind of rest cure; or because the business worker of the family has at last retired with money in the bank and can take all the time that is left to him in whatever way he will; or for some exceptional reason such as that which took Frank Cuppy and his daughter Ellen to sea. Young people cannot usually afford either time or money to travel by freighter; but toward the end of life, when one has less time, one has, strangely, more time.

A controlling factor that sometimes surprises passengers on a deep-sea freighter as they dilly-dally at wharves in foreign ports is that they – to whom stewards hasten, who are cosseted and deluded into a sense of importance – are of no importance whatever, and their movements are conditioned entirely by the freight which the ship will pick up or deposit in these foreign ports; and the movement of freight is conditioned by economic variations in different countries, by trade unions, or local flare-ups of policy or passion, or quarantine, or climate, and there is no guarantee whatever that the passengers will arrive at their ultimate destination at any given time. They discover that they are unimportant and are only the pawns of the tinned fruit and grain and borax, which are important. They find the sensation pleasant, and are surprised.

And so, as Ellen and her father leaned on the rail in the sunshine at the Oakland pier and watched nothing happening for a day or two, and then, as the longshoremen began to show their slow-motion effective activity, they insensibly entered the life of the freighter where all personal responsibilty ceases, and the period of private arrangements and decisions slides into the past.

Major Raymond Clark was fortunate in that he had two months' leave before taking up his new post at Ankara. He was a restless man, a congenital bachelor, a talker, a teaser, and well equipped to make a young girl pleased or uncomfortable. The three remaining empty places at the table promised possibilities of variety from this nice father and child who seemed rather gloomy and did not rise to his jokes very freely. He went out on deck and sauntered to and fro looking for someone to talk to.

Mrs. Gracey came on board at San Francisco as did many others, and at first the decks and lounge were full of people of both sexes who might be new passengers or the friends of passengers. The feeling that these people gave Ellen was that they were more exotic than people at home in British Columbia, but she was not familiar with that word.

Mrs. Gracey was very tired indeed. She had insisted on these weeks of rest before the opening of the Spring collections in Paris, and she did not propose to speak one word to one person all down the Pacific and across the Atlantic.

Mr. Bird, who had vineyards and a winery south of San Francisco, was affluent and had arrived at that place in life when he and his wife could take long trips during the year, which they did. He seemed to have no objection at all to Mrs. Bird talking all the time, or at least whenever possible.

Frank Cuppy was pleased that this woman Mrs. Gracey did not appear to need conversation, and it was not until Raymond Clark with all his clatter and questions had made the discovery that both François Cuppy and Nicola Gracey owed their Christian names to the interior of British Columbia that he felt the least interest in his table companion. Then they both became interested to the point of unexpected discovery and began to talk freely. Mrs. Gracey became quiet again, but a mutual feeling had been established and advanced. Happily she did not wish to be entertained. Ellen liked Mrs. Gracey very well, much better than Mrs. Bird, but was of opinion that they all sat too long over meals and all this talk was boring and some of it was lousy.

"May I be excused?" she said like a little girl. Everybody said Yes, and she went.

An intimacy grows when people share three meals a day, one soup, one afternoon tea, and several drinks, walks on deck, swimming and drying in the sun, lying in deck chairs in the warm evening – long hours are spent together each day for about thirty consecutive days from nine in the morning until midnight in the peculiar isolation of a ship at sea, where only a distant steamer occasionally intrudes afar off upon the empty waters, or a brightly coloured port is reached. "Come on, Miss Cuppy, shake a leg," said Major Clark and woke Ellen lying asleep in the sun to go swimming.

"Yes, I think you were quite right, France," said Mrs.

Gracey quietly in the dark to Frank Cuppy, "it was the best solution."

Ellen leaned on the high rail looking down on the swimming pool. It was the sailors' hour for swimming. How well they dived and swam, flashing over and under each other but not colliding in the small air and water space. The bosun's grandson edged along the pool holding on to the rope. He was timid. One day Mrs. Gracey said, "What is your name?" and he answered childishly, "I sea-boy, sea-boy I." A big bronze sailor teased him and pulled him into the water, but the bosun's grandson could not swim and went under among the arms and legs and bodies. Another sailor roughly and good-naturedly pulled him out and urged him to swim, but he climbed on to the surround of the pool and sat there shivering. He did not like to go away, he would be teased; he was afraid to go in; he was afraid of all the strong bodies swimming like torpedoes, diving like swallows, like bullets, safe in the water. He was afraid of the bronze boy who reached up and pulled his feet and his ankles and would not leave him alone.

"Oh, he's *mean*, the bully, you're *mean*!" cried Ellen, angry for the bosun's boy. He was beautiful, and pitiful, too, crouching there with all the big strong seamen so much older, shouting and diving and swimming. But however loud Ellen called, no one could hear above the lashing of the beautiful waves and the loud spill of water out of the swimming pool.

"He gives me the heaves, that feller, I seen him do that before," said an elderly man beside her.

The sun shone, the blue sea rose and fell, the curling waves assailed the ship pleasantly, the diving sea-boys laughed and shouted and the bosun's grandson crouched above the water.

"A Botticelli angel in bathing trunks," said Mrs. Gracey beside Ellen, "poor child."

The sailors left the pool, the passengers clambered down and in slower tempo dived and swam, all except Ellen who dived like a scarlet and brown arrow, and did the crawl faster and faster, getting in people's way and apologizing. She thought of the bosun's boy, and wondered whether, when he put his shirt and pants on again, the sailor still teased him. She hoped not. That sailor was lousy. Down she flashed into the pool and scrambled up again.

It was hard to believe that the next day was Christmas Eve, and the sun today so hot and the last of the porpoises rolling and tumbling and leaping through the waves. The voyage on the freighter had proved successful. A stranger would think Frank Cuppy remarkably recovered and brown and handsome; Ellen glowed with something like beauty; Mrs. Gracey was quiet as always (but responsive) and no longer showed fatigue; no one would notice Major Clark in any case. The days were slipping past. At night, while Ellen danced, Frank Cuppy walked with Mrs. Gracey in the warm night, talking and not talking. Sometimes they stopped to lean on the rail and look down at the phosphorescence in the black ocean. Sometimes, but rarely – when he could bring himself to do so – Frank spoke of Susan, for Mrs. Gracey was an understanding woman who did not feel it necessary to embarrass by words.

Frank was at times beset by the uneasy feeling that he – and Ellen – were too readily trying to oblige Susan by being happy. The thought was crude, but it persisted, and then retreated. He did not know what Ellen thought, or *if* she thought, or biddably obeyed her father's words. He did not know which was permanently valid – the cruel sense of eternal bereavement which had possessed the young girl and himself, or this gradual acceptance and readjustment to finality which came of sun, sea, isolation, and companionship. Susan was present. She was gone. He was confused. The ship was real and present. So were the passengers.

Ellen was sometimes assailed by awareness of the guilt of forgetting. She prayed at night to her mother. "Oh Mother, never leave me though we dance and swim and Father talks to Mrs. Gracey."

Yet Father could do no other. Could they change their table places? Could they avoid Mrs. Gracey, toward whom Ellen had begun to develop a faint, a very faint animosity? Mrs. Gracey was nice. She took people or left them alone. Ellen, helpless and solitary, looked to see if Mrs. Gracey were trying to attract Father. Honestly, she did not think so but she did not know enough to know.

Something, thought Mrs. Gracey, is going to happen. If the voyage ends too soon, France will say goodbye, and all this is over. If I do not press, something is going to happen. If I press, it will not happen. It may not happen yet. Poor France, she thought, poor Ellen. Her life is before her and soon she won't need him any more and there's that older sister. I need him, very much, more than any of them. Mrs. Gracey could easily harden herself to Ellen and to Susan. It will be better for France, she thought, and I could be very happy with him, and no harm done to Susan. I never knew her but she is important to me and I have nothing against her but I must match her. Mrs. Gracey was not unkind but she was a gently determined woman. It had not taken her two weeks to make up her mind.

On Christmas Eve the Chief Steward escorted Mrs. Gracey, Ellen, Major Clark and Frank Cuppy to the large mess room where the sailors sang. It was a pity that the sea had risen and a strong wind was blowing. There was more motion of the ship.

Ten

"I think that I shall never see
A face so like a chimpanzee,"

whispered Susan in her light voice with her little splutter of laughter. "Do look at Mr. Magnus! No, not the sailors . . . There's no doubt, Frank, that the human face . . . " she whispered. But it could not be Susan, for Susan was not there.

There was certainly a very strange and enclosed feeling in the mess room. The sea had grown much rougher and there was no longer the sensation of travelling smoothly to which they had become accustomed. The room was almost dark but gradually eyes became used to what light there was. The light came from small globes decorating the Christmas tree which stood crowded into the corner. It was a fairly large fir tree and it must have been brought on board with Christmas in mind, either in British Columbia or Oregon or even California. There was a light, too, over the orchestra, in which there were five players. All instruments except the two mouth-organs were home-made. An orange-haired boy in a yellow shirt open from neck to navel fingered a wooden flute. A sailor plucked tentatively at the strings of a wooden and stringed guitar or mandoline or lute. In the centre of the players sat a young seaman who held a tall percussion instrument sternly, fondly, and the instrument was made of a biscuit tin, a clapper, and a long leather thong. Each player bent like a lover to his instrument.

The sailors, sitting crowded in the near-dark on long benches beside the mess tables, straddling sideways, all turned one way, faced and gazed seriously upon the musicians. There was no laughing or high spirits. The flute sounded, the musicians swayed to their music and in the shadows the seamen began to sing loudly in unison. Broken light fell on the stern faces of the young sailors, proclaiming brows, eye sockets, the planes of cheek-bone and jaw and strong throats. The seamen drank between songs from the one only twinkling green glass bottle of Christmas beer that each held in his hand. The strong voices sounded in unison in these unknown hymns and songs, the players closed their eyes and bent like lovers to their instruments, the ship shuddered and plunged, for the wind had risen noticeably. The few passengers squeezed into the mess room were onlookers only, and superfluous.

Why don't they laugh and sing, I think they must be singing hymns, thought Ellen, wondering, and remembering the laughing swimmers. The sailors sang song after song, verse after verse, like hymns. There was the strange feeling of this room, this cave in the ocean full of sound, the sea beating on the ship, and the great dark unknown fish around and beneath the ship. Frank Cuppy at last bowed his face to his hands as if to listen. Something unbearable was happening to him and it was something that could not be true. Beside him he was aware of Susan who said in her light earnest voice, "Oh Frank, isn't it wonderful! I never in all my life felt anything like this – all those singing boys and the sea rushing... oh Frank, what fun to be here together!" and as always she slipped her arm through his; and at his other side, touching him with her hand, Nicola Gracey whispered, "Look, France, there's the Botticelli babe, the seaboy!" but he did not hear what she said. He groaned in his spirit, but of course Susan was not really there. He had lost her again.

The bosun's boy gazed in wonder at the singing sailors and at the Christmas tree and at the passengers in their rather evening dress. His eyes shone wide like a child's shining eyes and his lips were open. This is wonderful, thought Susan's daughter, I never in all my life saw anything like this – all these boys singing and the sea rushing . . . She sat crowded between Nicola Gracey and Major Raymond Clark. The place grew hot; the motion of the ship was increasing; the roar of the waves and the songs of the seamen filled the mess room. They seemed as if they would never stop singing.

"Let us go," said Frank Cuppy suddenly, and, at the next pause, as the music for a moment ceased, they got up and thanking and thanking they made their way through the stewards in the galley and the sonorous singing broke out afresh and followed them to the stair head.

"I'm going to bed, what about you, Gyp?" Father said harshly and abruptly. "You'd better come, it's getting rough. Come on, kid", and he turned and went down the companion-way to his cabin, followed by Ellen who said Good-night over her shoulder. He left without saying a word to his companions, not even Good-night.

"Feeling the motion," said Raymond Clark to Mrs. Gracey. "Come on up to the lounge. This calls for a drink."

It is probable that the effect of the seamen's singing was so powerful because the passengers did not understand the words. What were the words? There was no meaning for the passengers, and no meaning was needed, only the passion and vigour and the sound of the singing in unison in that cave of the sea.

Eleven

NEXT MORNING the storm had abated a little, but the ocean was of a curious lion colour, not to be trusted. It did not seem possible that the water could be tawny, but the sky was peculiar in appearance and that may have been the reason. A passenger walking on the south deck beheld in the distance, near the horizon or so it seemed, a waterspout. Everyone gathered at the rail edge and soon the waterspout was joined by two other waterspouts. They were nearer now, and gave an effect of irresistible force as their columns wavered slightly but curved and straightened up to join the sky. This remarkable sight caused great satisfaction to the passengers since the waterspouts, which were irresponsible, kept their distance and showed no signs of approaching and descending upon the ship. "Like tigers at a safe distance," said Ellen to her father. The passengers were further reassured since the storm of last night was left behind, it seemed, and with a calmer sea and relatively good weather they re-established themselves. "Who'll play shuffleboard?" (of which everyone was tired) they said as the waterspouts fell away. The sailors were busy dismantling the swimming pool with great speed. In the early afternoon the wind freshened.

The afternoon could not be said to be enjoyable. The wind rose with a sense of unlimited power. The waves were of a new dimension, very high and deep, and assailed the ship. Orders were given that the passengers should not go out on deck. This was supposed to be Christmas Day but did not behave accordingly. Stewards put fiddles on the tables. No one was really amused when Mr. Magnus went about with a piece of synthetic mistletoe which he had kept specially for the occasion, and tried to kiss the ladies. The swimming pool was down, one supposed, and the sailors were seen indistinctly by passengers looking through portholes, beating their way against wind and spray, engaged in essential tasks of which the passengers knew nothing, their trousers whipping against their legs, their heads bent to the storm. The day became dark too early owing to the blackness of the sky. The motion of the ship was jerky and violent, and many people wished they had never put to sea. A few passengers only remained in the lounge and behaved in a suitably convivial manner. No one drank much, however, because the difficulty of staying on one's feet was almost too great and alcohol was superfluous. Outside the portholes now there was only blackness. The wind was terrific. By this time many of the passengers decided to have Christmas dinner, if any, in bed. Raymond Clark helped an elderly woman down to her cabin and, as he returned to join the others, he shot across the lounge, cut his head against a table, and was seasick.

Frank Cuppy and the bar steward and two other men removed Major Clark to his cabin, staggering along with difficulty ("Stay where you are, Gyp," said her father), and Nicola Gracey followed with care. The bar steward sent the cabin steward for the doctor, as Major Clark's cut was four inches long and too deep for safety and he seemed stunned. The doctor could not come, as a seaman had fallen from some height to the deck and had received multiple fractures.

Nicola Gracey and the cabin steward did the best they could for Major Clark, and Frank returned, clutching and staggering, to Ellen who was sitting on the floor so as not to fall. The lights in the lounge – which was deserted – flickered uncertainly.

"Come, Gyp – one two three, there we go," said Father cheerfully, and together they went down to Gypsy's cabin, and Father helped her to bed.

"Stay there, kid," he said, "and then I'll know you're safe.

And don't be scared. . . . I've been in lots worse storms than this" (that was not true). "How d'you feel?"

"I feel all right," said Gypsy smiling hard, but she felt very queer; not seasick, not exactly frightened although on the brink of being frightened, very much excited, very much alone on this sea, and yet very much together with all the other people who were also alone.

"Now you're all right, Gyp," said Father, "stay there and don't move. . . . we don't want any broken bones in our family. Got a book?" (Who could read a book in all that gallimaufry of assault and lurch, shudder and roar; the waves assaulted the ship with continuous thunder, the wind was deafening, the ship struggled and plunged, with a sideways shake, and seemed suddenly insignificant upon the ocean.)

"Yes," said Ellen, determinedly well and cheerful. "See, I have a novel. I won't move, Daddy, dear Daddy! Go back to Major Clark . . . " and Father looked back from the door and saw Ellen sitting up in bed like a good girl with her novel on the blanket. He hoped that she would not shoot out of her bunk on to the floor. Everything slid and fell.

"I'll be back," he said. "Ring for the steward if you want him", and he hooked the door open, and left her.

It was a good thing that the passengers were not told, and did not know, that the bosun's boy, who had been instructed to stay within and then was forgotten, had slipped out with the sailors and had been stripped off the deck like a leaf and flung into the dark.

I sea-boy, sea-boy I.

Twelve

WORD FILTERED through the ship that the wind had reached sixty miles an hour, eighty, ninety miles. Someone said the cargo must have shifted. Ellen gripped the side of her berth and stayed in it wedged tight. Father and Mrs. Gracey and a Mr. Macdonald who was not seasick went into the seamen's quarters and helped the ship's surgeon. A seaman who had been ill became delirious, and had to be controlled, and there were one or two scalp wounds. One of the cabin stewards was hurled against a wall and broke his collar-bone. There were only minor injuries amongst the passengers, most of whom were in bed.

At about eight-thirty Ellen heard a new sound enter. The ocean, flung in a huge wave against the ship, broke open double doors on to a deck and poured in, cataracting down the stairs and companion-ways. There was rushing and trampling, a bringing of wood and carpenter's helpers, a turning – perhaps of the ship – a hammering, and the sea ceased to break through. The ship was certainly attacked by the mad ocean.

Ellen heard a woman in hysteria. "We are going down. Oh God, we're going down," she wailed.

Ellen then heard her father's voice, sharp and reassuring, "Nonsense! This ship has been through dozens of worse gales than this. Where's your cabin? And don't . . ."

Father's voice was drowned by noise and Ellen supposed

that he had escorted the passenger to bed. He had probably slapped her.

Father came into the cabin. He looked cheerful. You would think he enjoyed the storm, but no one could do that. The sight of Father made Ellen feel better.

"You all right, Gypsy?" he said. "I'm going along to see Clark . . ."

"Can't I come and help?" said Ellen.

"No, you stay put." Father was in unusually good humour. "We're going down to the fo'c'sle again, lots of cuts and abrasions and the doctor's single-handed. G'bye."

"Oh, let me go, let me help!" Ellen saw herself in a new and pleasing rôle, and, also, she honestly wanted to help. What a missed opportunity.

"You'd only be in the way," said her father curtly. "The wind's dying down now" (the wind and sea pounded the ship harder than ever), "but you're better where you are."

". . . is Mrs. Gracey going?" asked Ellen.

"Yes, she's good", and her father left her.

Perhaps Father had not meant that Mrs. Gracey was "good", she might not be good at all, but she might be good at this kind of thing. Ellen, holding on to the side of her berth and a strap on the wall (her novel had long since fallen to the floor), pictured Mrs. Gracey with great dislike as an imitation heroine, "going among the injured", the sneaky thing, raising herself thereby in Father's estimation.

Mrs. Gracey, who had once been trained in a hospital but had almost forgotten the fact, went among the injured with a dangerous feeling of nausea and was frightened by the storm but supported by the cheerful presence of Frank Cuppy; she did her best, stumbling along companion-ways, coming up short against walls, keeping her feet; she was tired; she looked plain and sick, and would have preferred to be in bed, but she was useful.

"Mrs. Gracey is a very bad influence on Father," Ellen said aloud sanctimoniously, "she's taking a mean advantage."

At that moment the ship shuddered violently. The last and greatest of a succession of battering waves blew in Ellen's porthole, which flew across the end of the cabin like a giant monocle, followed by the dark ocean.

Thirteen

BEFORE ELLEN could decide what she must do (she shrank against the wall) the ship had reeled one way, and back, and a column of water rushed in again, spreading over the floor, rising. A cabin steward, dodging, drenched, snatched the girl in her blanket from the bed, carried her to her father's cabin, deposited her on his bed, and left her. There was rushing and trampling, a bringing of great discs of wood and stanchions, a turning – perhaps – of the ship, a hammering in of the great discs of wood (three portholes were blown) and Ellen got into her father's bed. She, miraculously, was not very wet, yet her teeth chattered and she shivered with cold and excitement. She lay in Father's bed for hours, or so it seemed. It appeared that the storm was abating, but as soon as she thought that the storm was abating, fresh gusts arose. But, certainly, the storm had diminished. Time passed.

Where is he? I must find him, thought Ellen.

She got up and wrapped herself in a blanket. She went carefully along the companion-way, steadying herself as she went. She climbed the stairs. The hands of the clock on the wall showed half-past three. A hurrying steward saw her, hesitated, waved cheerfully and went on his way.

I will look in the lounge, in case, she said to herself, because she did not know where else to look. She pulled the blanket up so that she would not trip, and made a little run across to the entrance of the lounge, supporting herself there.

Only a few lights were still on in the lounge. There seemed

to be no one there. Ellen, entering, holding on to the doorway and clutching her blanket, looked around the large cabin.

On the long padded seat surrounding the room sat her father and Mrs. Gracey. His legs were sprawled out in front of him. His head was inclined on his chest toward Mrs. Gracey's head which lay lower on his shoulder. Her face was turned up toward the dim light. She was not at first recognizable because her face was so pale and plain and her large dark eyes were closed. She looked tousled and weary, as of course she was. Father's arm was round her. Ellen, wrapped up in her blanket at the door, saw that Father and Mrs. Gracey were fast asleep.

Fourteen

NEXT DAY a certain esprit de corps made all the passengers pretend that the storm had not really been very bad. The passengers, pallid beneath their tan, arose gradually, languidly, but with relief. No one mentioned the bosun's boy in public. Some thought that a fund should be collected and given to the child's grandfather for his mother. Others thought that a gift of money was not delicate. The cloud of the child's death hung over the whole ship from bow to stern. The question of the fund was left in the hands of Mr. Cuppy and Major Clark who emerged from his cabin with plasters on his head.

Ellen regarded her father and Mrs. Gracey with shock and fear. Mrs. Gracey was quiet. Father was as gloomy as when he boarded the ship. He was not even nice to Mrs. Gracey. It was not Frank Cuppy's way to dissemble his feelings, and he was singularly unaware of himself, either as a handsome man, an absorbed man, a desirable man, a temporarily agreeable man or a gloomy man. If he felt gloomy, he was gloomy, and to hell with the people who happened to be around. They were almost not there.

Mrs. Bird said to Mr. Bird after lunch, "Say, what's wrong with France Cuppy? He never said a word all lunch-time."

"Maybe she turned him down."

"Not she."

Nicola Gracey was aware of France's bad humour but was pleased. Evidently what he had said to her when they went upstairs after that awful night had disturbed him, and she was satisfied that he should be disturbed. She comported herself as usual and by afternoon France seemed to feel better. They walked several times round the deck and then she said she was going below for a rest. She did not press her advantage.

Ellen had prayed to her mother in that early morning, "Mother, Mother, whatever shall we do?" but there was nothing to do.

So they had come full circle again, yet to a lower place. They had embarked nearly five weeks ago – four months after Mother's funeral which seemed just to have happened – with the simple and noble grief of bereavement. They had become eased, and happy (to a point, at least), and now something that was not simple and noble but again unhappy had come upon them separately and together. Ellen, fiddling about in her cabin, was aware of a shadow, a smudge, as of betrayals. She did not know what was right, and to whom, or what was wrong, and to whom. She was too inexperienced and solitary. She was caught on a margin of innocence and surprise. Sleeping together had a meaning beyond itself. They were certainly sleeping together but not in any shameful way. Yet they were sleeping together and Father's arm was round her, her hand was in his, and her head . . . it was offensive to the young girl that two old people (well, nearly old – strangers, she said, her anger rising) should behave like that. She was bewildered, deeply offended, and dismayed. She could not enquire of her mother. If Nora had been there, she would not have talked to Nora about this new thing that had come upon them, too soon, and had so greatly offended her. That was the grief; it was too soon; and Father seemed to be deep in it. To talk, even to Isa, would be betrayal.

Passengers began to speak of destinations and hotels.

"We shall go direct to Perris," announced Mrs. Bird, "I'm crazy about Perris. Mr. Bird always says Let's try somewhere else but I always say give me two weeks in Perris and then I'll go anywhere for anybody. Mr. Bird got our reservations at the Grand Hotel months ago."

Mrs. Gracey was also going to Paris, but only for a few

days and not to the Grand Hotel but to some little hotel she knew. She said, vaguely, that she might then go to London.

Mr. Cuppy and his daughter were going to London, but only for a short time as Ellen had to return home to school.

Major Clark was going to London and would then make his way to Ankara.

Like migrating birds delayed, the passengers twittered and became fidgety. The voyage had lasted too long.

Fifteen

"I HAD AN airmail from Gypsy today. At last," said Nora. "It was posted in Antwerp."

"Well, you know, dolling, it couldn't have been mailed before they got to Antwerp. Have they had a good time?"

"They were delayed," said Nora. "They had a storm. They should be in London now. I'll read it to you. No, I don't seem to think they did have a good time. You'll see what you think. She's usually so . . . so . . . "

"Exuberant," said Morgan.

"Dear Nora

We have been delayed a lot at every port I think I told you because of strikes and things. We had a bad storm they said it was ninety miles an hour. A little sailor was drowned at sea. It was terrible and everyone felt awful. We land tomorrow but this letter will be taken into Antwerp by the pilot boat tonight. It will be just lovely to see you again I simply can't wait. I think if its all the same to you I'd like to board with the other girls at May Cross and come to you and Isa at weekends. I've thought about it a lot and I think that would be lovely if its all the same to you. How is Morgan. I could come home by boat but I don't want to be on the sea any more just now so I shall fly home. I will write to you from London. Dear Nora it will be lovely to see you again.

        Lots of love, Gypsy."

"She doesn't mention Father," said Nora, raising her eyes to her husband, "and she doesn't say they had a good time. I call that a stiff letter, and childish."

"Homesick," said Morgan.

"Well, we'll soon hear from London. They should be there now." But they were not.

The Scheldt river is wide but the navigable channel is narrow. The sands shift and endanger vessels. Shortly after the pilot came aboard, the freighter hit a sandbar, thrashed about, and settled gently and firmly at a slant. It was a strange feeling, sinking gently into the sand. The passengers had packed and, wearing urban clothes, adjusted themselves to the slope of the vessel. They did not blame the captain or the pilot so they blamed the sands of the river. They did not like the tilt of the vessel.

Mr. Harris knew of a ship that struck a sandbar in the Scheldt river and broke her back, losing half of the crew. Mr. Macdonald remembered the incident distinctly and others. Sandbars, which had previously been non-existent, became notoriously dangerous. How ridiculous to weather that storm and then perish on a sandbar. The wind rose but died again. Spirits became low. Large freighters of all nations and some dirty English coalers sped rapidly up and down the river channel past them as they lay at an angle on the left bank of the river, like lepers avoided.

Two large tugs came out from Antwerp, then five, seven, ten. After two days and nights, at a right conjunction of wind and tide, the tugs manoeuvred the ship off the sandbar and the passengers rejoiced, only to find that the ship was back to front. There was not room to turn in the channel of the river without the danger of becoming expensively stuck again. As the ship's nose was pointed out to sea, whence she had come, she headed there, downstream. As she headed downstream a fog descended and by the time the ship neared Flushing the fog was dense, and there they lay in fog for two days. The delay exasperated everyone. Then, when the fog cleared somewhat, they headed upstream again. As time went on, some people became too involved with each other, and many persons showed a tendency to get drunk.

Sixteen

THEY ARRIVED in London.

Ellen's one idea now was to get home as quickly as possible and become a boarder with the other girls at May Cross School. She had spent her sixteen years in the company of her mother who had a light and pleasant sense of the ridiculous. Life with her mother had been amusing and there had been a lot of laughter. Mother picked pretty pebbles off the beach of life and they sparkled gaily everywhere; a great deal of quotation without inverted commas. It was much easier to be quiet and not bother Mother when she said "Oh Gypsy, do be quiet, can't you see I'm thinking about my education?" than if Mother had said "*Can't* you keep quiet?" Father was important to her and serious. Nora was important to her. She was a good sister but had no sense of humour. There was no laughing anywhere and there seemed to be nothing to laugh about now. Gypsy could hardly wait to get back to Isa and all the others at May Cross.

Her time in London was short. Father had to see some men at once, but he found time to go with Gypsy to a famous shop where they bought a tweed suit and coat and hat. She was so slim that she was easy to fit. Gypsy cheered up enormously when she put on her new suit and Mrs. Gracey then ceased to prey upon her so much. Major Clark, who stayed at their hotel, took her to the Abbey and to some matinées, and she and Father and Major Clark went on the razzle-dazzle in the evenings. She forgot that she had ever not liked Major Clark.

When they went to the airport Ellen wore her new suit and hat with a red silk scarf. She looked lovely. Major Clark said in his silly way, "Gentlemen can't give jewellery to ladies unless they are engaged to be married to them so I have brought you this magnificent bracelet", and he gave her a silver bracelet with every kind of small beautiful silver toy dangling from it. On the plane Ellen would be able to turn it over and scrutinize the shoe, the ship, the teapot, the little dog and cat, and never be bored by the infinite sky. "Oh Major Clark, how *sweet* you are!" she said ecstatically.

Major Clark was not as silly as he seemed, or he would not have been sent to Ankara. He said, quietly, "Goodbye, Miss Cuppy. Now keep your chin up", and then went to look at some maps on the waiting-room wall.

Father said, "I've told the stewardess to look after you. Let's see your tickets again . . . don't forget and put your handbag down."

"Oh no, I won't, Father," said Ellen earnestly, "my beautiful new bag!"

The tall father and his young daughter stood together looking into each other's faces; if there were any tears, they were hidden from each other. Mother . . . a wisp of anxiety, a wisp of appeasement . . . was there, and a brown-eyed shade that was Mrs. Gracey about to arrive in London passed and repassed. Ellen's heart said, Father . . . whatever you do . . . it's all right whatever you do . . . but what her heart would say aloud her mind forbade her tongue to utter.

"Happy landings, Gyp," said Father.

She flung her arms round her father's neck saying, "Goodbye, Daddy, dear *dear* Daddy", she was suddenly so sorry for him. He stood looking after her and waving as she turned to wave, standing for a moment at the open door of the plane.

In her much later life the long period which elapsed between the voyage and the meeting with her husband at the railway station seemed – erroneously – to Ellen to have passed with the fluidity and the sometimes violence of dreams, and therefore to be of no true significance. It is a fact that to one person a voyage may mean only a departure and an arrival, an expense incurred, only a happy lapse of coloured time, only an embarking and a disembarking – the distance between two places on a map which may be pink or even blue; but to Ellen the voyage was a shaking and transforming experience with which nothing in her future personal life was comparable, not even the events of the war because she was only one of millions of participants, and certainly not the years during which she worked for old Mr. Platt in Saskatoon – until she met George on the railway platform, and for the duration of her life thereafter. There is a curious semblance of reality in those of our years which are certainly valid, but seem to elide, and differ from our years of reality. During those years of elision we live, of course, with relative intensity, and those years mark, retard, hasten, improve, or worsen us, and, alas, may affect some of those with whom we come into touch to a degree of pleasure, exasperation or even of damage, of which we are only partly aware; but then the true years of our life arrive – or do not arrive – and we forget those other irrelevant years which may, since Time is an agent, some day stir, and take their unexpected vengeance in a variety of ingenious ways. Such, at least, was Ellen's experience.

PART TWO

A Few Years

Seventeen

SOON AFTER Ellen returned from the voyage on which her father met Mrs. Gracey whom he subsequently married, Nora's first baby, a boy, was born, and died.

While Ellen was still in Quebec in training as a Wren, before she went overseas, Nora's second child, also a boy, was born. He was deformed, and a mongol. Aunt Maury Peake wrote to Ellen and told her this very bad news, adding: "I think if I were you I'd make only the barest mention of this in writing to Nora. She is apathetic, and who can wonder, after everything, and wishes no comment or reference. The baby has been sent to a suitable place in the country to good people. If it hadn't been for the loss of the first baby, Nora would have been able to cope perhaps. It seems better for her to forget if she can for the time being, seeing it has hit her so awfully hard. She doesn't seem able to face it at all." So Ellen also forgot, or nearly forgot, in the immediacy of things. She felt desperately sorry for Nora, at the time, and of no use to her.

When Ellen was stationed in the Haymarket and the buzz-bombs were falling on London, Nora's third – and last – child was born. It was Aunt Maury who wrote (Nora had become a somewhat indifferent correspondent): "After all the cares and fears, Nora has a beautiful boy. He is a cherub", and later: "Nora has come to life. The cherub becomes more cherubic. She is completely wrapped up in him, and can see nothing else. She is well, and rejuvenated", but . . . what Aunt Maury did not say was that no woman should dare to be absorbed in her child as Nora was absorbed in her son. Aunt Maury wrote out of the depths of her knowledge of the love and despair and loss of a child. One son was in Egypt, one boy was invalided home, and Billy, her eldest, was lost at sea.

When Ellen returned home to Vancouver after the war, there was still no mention by anyone of the second son. Morgan and the returning Gypsy were only vehicles, it seemed, for the expression of praise and discovery and love of the beautiful baby around whom the house spun smoothly.

Ellen, looking about her, took a small flat. She completed an interrupted course in shorthand and typing. She worked one evening a week among children at a Neighbourhood House. She began to ride again, and to play badminton and tennis with old friends, new friends. Huw Peake, who was Morgan Peake's young step-brother and lived with his mother in Toronto, came west for the purpose of being articled to Morgan and entering his office. Huw had been for three and a half years a prisoner of war. That is a fearful thing. They may find him a little difficult at first, thought his mother uneasily, but she did not say so to Morgan to whom she wrote volubly. She had confidence in Morgan because he was so much older than Huw and (she had reason to think) kind.

"Why do they spell it Huw?" asked Ellen. "It looks like a Dobermann Pinscher, ending off so short, without a tail."

"Welsh," said Nora absently. "Oh look, look, isn't he adorable?" "Yes," said Ellen, smiling at the cherub.

Huw and Ellen met and fell in love. They became engaged and people said how suitable it was.

Eighteen

LYING FLAT on her back at two o'clock in the morning, Ellen reflected upon the nature of reality, which she found to be one (or almost one) with the nature of light – light implying, of course, also the absence of light; that is, darkness.

This was because the ceiling of her bedroom at which she looked, while being in its own nature a white ceiling, was dark, since the night was dark. But a light in the street below made the ceiling partially pale, luminous, and – intercepted as the light was by a space of wall between her two windows and by other obstacles which Ellen could not quite determine – the light and the darkness between them made stationary patterns upon the ceiling, so that curious irregular wedge-shaped quadrilaterals of light and dark lay there in a design of great beauty which Ellen thought of, wrongly, as an arabesque. Some overlay others, rendering them light as seen through a veil, or dark as seen through a veil. There slid continuously along the ceiling from left to right, toward the open windows, uniform rectangles of moving light which passed, sliding, followed by other rectangles of light which also slid away. These were the counterpart in light of the displacement and the noise of cars which passed below the windows and disappeared, taking their noise with them.

In time to come, Ellen could not look up and see such a pattern of still light and dark, and of light moving across the pattern, without remembering that, whatever there was on the ceiling, she lay there saying to herself with growing conviction No, I cannot marry Huw, it would be the greatest mistake. We might be happy sometimes but we would nearly always be unhappy. What a life together! He is bad-tempered, I know that now. It's not only that dark cross look (which is very handsome), he is really bad-tempered. And then from the area of love and compassion would come the unsure statement No, no; it was that long time that he was a prisoner of war; how can I break our engagement because he was a prisoner of war and became bad-tempered? That is too cruel; it is very base and I would always be ashamed to have done such a thing. But from the area of Ellen's common sense rose a conviction that, long before Huw had been taken prisoner, he had been a bad-tempered man and a bad-tempered boy. He was, in fact, bad-tempered by nature, and always would be, and not only because he had been a prisoner of war. This conviction made her say to herself (a little frightened) Tomorrow I shall tell him; well, if not tomorrow, the next day, or soon – I must tell him soon. She advised herself and two voices spoke, one saying, "An opportunity will arise – he will be bad-tempered again as he was today and then you can do it"; and the other voice said, "No, you will have to make your own opportunity; he may only be sulky again next time, and against sulkiness you have no defence."

Looking forward, Ellen saw with dismay the change-over from her being engaged to marry Huw who was Morgan's step-brother and Nora's brother-in-law and accepted with her by everyone, to a person who has broken faith with a man, close in the circle of family and friends, who was, so recently and for so long, a prisoner of war.

At least she was alone now – lying and looking up at the rectangles of light and dark gliding strangely across the pattern of the ceiling – and conforming to no one. If she continued in this engagement she would never be alone like this, possessing herself, making up her mind about things. From another place issued a thought – whether unworthy or merely truthful, she did not know – that there was something in herself that provoked Huw's ill-nature to the point that he would be very much relieved if she should say goodbye.

Such a number of things arise between two people, she thought, looking up at the rectangles which continued gliding across and out, which onlookers do not know; and so, perhaps, if I say to Huw at some time – better sooner than late – that we are not suited ("I am suited", "I find I am not suited", said the applicant), he may be very glad, and glad also that I have done that, and have not waited for him to drive me to tears, or to the obstinacy or courage required in a marriage of which one is not sure. If one could only read the other's true mind, she thought with real distress, if there were only no mistrust, no veil between, no inability to discover why one is annoying and the other is bad-tempered. Dear Huw, she thought with a rush of affection, I must not let myself love you because (I know) we are not suited, but I must bear the reasonable blame of having broken my engagement with one who has been so long and so lately a prisoner of war, and close in the family; and she could hear the voices of friends and acquaintances: "My dear, it is really awful for him, he was a prisoner of war; he's had enough to bear, she should have been more patient. The Morgan Peakes will be terribly upset."

I will go away, she thought, probably to Saskatoon, and stay for a while with Mary Ford, I mean Mary Livingstone. That will be the best thing. She refused to go over the arguments again, although it was difficult to stop.

It was nearly dawn time and she became aware, still looking up, that while she had argued and come to her decision (of which she was still very much afraid although there was somewhere an element of intense relief), the wedge shapes of light and dark and the sliding rectangles had almost disappeared, wiped out by the general dawn. What happens to them? Are they still there but in the presence of light do we not see them? The thought alarmed her – what is around us? She did not at that moment think that there was somewhere some parallel of light and darkness, of illumination and blotting-out, and perhaps our whole existence, one with another, is a trick of light. That may be somewhere near the truth, which is often hard to determine because of the presence of the lights and shadows of look, word, thought which touch, glide, pass or remain. Sometimes the light falls, and rests, with a beautiful clarity, and truth lies clear. That was the case with Ellen and her great friend Isa Graham who now was Isa Cheney and lived in the Okanagan, and with Isa's husband Charles, and it had always been so with her mother and with Billy Peake who was lost at sea, and with his mother Aunt Maury. But with Huw and Ellen the light did not fall clear; the marriage would never do. (What did Huw think? Nothing. He did not look forward ever, but took each day as it came. He was brave, stubborn, honest and easily annoyed, and always had been easily annoyed. Aunt Maury Peake could have told Ellen that for she had known him when he was a boy. But one does not tell these things to newly affianced people. One dare not. It is dangerous – but then, most things are dangerous. Nothing is safe.)

Nineteen

ON THE next day when Huw picked her up at her little flat, Ellen was apprehensive. She would follow the advice of the moment as it came, but she wished the evening over, and the avowal, and the explanations if any, and the parting. But Huw was amiable, and, as they had dinner together and she looked at his dark face across the table, she knew that she did not entirely wish to leave him. He had a sceptical look. He was not particularly sceptical, but the look was strong on his face; yet when he smiled, his smile was a surprise, and engaging.

"I suppose we'd better go tomorrow and get it over," he said. "It's idiotic spending a whole afternoon in going to see people you don't give a hoot for."

Former acquaintances of his mother's called Ransome had bought a small farm up the Fraser Valley at Whonnock, and Mrs. Peake had written from Toronto that Mr. and Mrs. Ransome wanted Huw to take Ellen to see them. That was the kind of thing his mother did. She too often took the whips of love to him. He disliked going to see these people, or any people, unless they were entirely congenial to him. He disliked driving all the way up the Valley merely to see these old forgotten Ransomes; but they must get it over, because his mother had written and would write again and again.

"When we are married," said Huw, fiddling with a spoon and looking quickly across at Ellen, "I hope you won't want to go visiting everyone who asks us. I like the ones I like but I hate like hell to have to see people I don't like."

"Don't you like the Ransomes?"

"Just for once and never again, and not tomorrow. Hardly remember them."

"But you can't cut *everyone* out because you don't entirely like them, Huw! You just *can't*!"

"Yes I can. Every one of them", and he drank his coffee. "Life is too short for Ransomes and stupid people. God, I've seen enough of stupid people to last me my time."

Ellen thought of her father. But her father's antipathy to people was not deliberate and he did not insist on your dislike of them too. Simply he did not observe them. This was different. An exclusion, an alignment was required by Huw. What kind of life were she and Huw to lead if they were going to like nobody but ten people, five people, themselves, Huw, and at last only a dog – perhaps? Was this worth speaking of now? Is this an issue? Her lips parted and she looked at Huw. No, he was not bad-tempered now. He was speaking the simple truth, mildly, despite the scowl which was, she decided, only a modelling of his face. I will not interfere. "Silly-Billy," she said, smiling at him.

"Come, darling," he said, getting up, "or we'll be late," and of course she could not speak now of breaking their engagement to anyone as sweet as Huw.

The next morning – Saturday – was overcast. Rain fell and became a downpour. If you are happy and in love, no drive is dreary. If you are not happy, and are wary and unsure, a drive up a valley dripping with rain is dreary, and silent (not with the silence that is better than speech) and – besides, Huw telephoned – the car had developed a knock in the engine.

"Oh, don't let's go!" exclaimed Ellen, relieved by the knock in the engine. "They'll have a telephone! Let's telephone . . ."

"And put it off! We're *going*; unless of course you don't *want* to go – I thought you were so keen on going . . . " And so on. There came a bickering. Ellen did not care if it rained, nor if there were a knock in the engine, nor if the Ransomes were as stupid as owls, but she did care that they should not, as so often, argue about nothing. Huw called for her, and they drove away in the rain. Rain obliterated the mountains, the sea, the river, the countryside. The knock in the car was irritating. After a few tries at speech, Ellen was silent. Anything she said was wrong. "A nice jaunt to the country," Mrs. Ransome had written in her note, prophetic with dullness. A nice jaunt to the country indeed! Ellen laughed.

Huw said, "What's funny?"

"Mrs. Ransome said we would have a nice jaunt to the country," she said, "and look at it!" (the rain lashed the car). "Do see it's funny, Huw!"

Huw grunted and Ellen fell silent again. They drove on.

So this is how it will be. If at this moment we were in danger, if – say – we were caught in a blizzard in the mountains, I believe that Huw would not be angry. He would walk, climb, carry, starve, with a kind of fierce joy, but he wouldn't complain. I am sure of it. But our life will not consist of crises in blizzards in mountains; it will be just this – the Ransomes, the rain, a knock in the engine, Ellen being annoyingly reasonable, or silent, or unsympathetic, but always wrong – always trying to adjust herself, and always failing. Huw doesn't know about "other people", she thought, and I can do nothing about *that*. So they drove, Huw impatient with those things that made him impatient – the Ransomes, the rain, the wasted Saturday afternoon. It did not even require the knock in the engine. That was thrown in, a bonus. He did not really think about Ellen sitting there quite blotted out by the Ransomes, the rain, and the knock in the engine. She was there; that was good enough. They lost their way.

The country road that turns up the hill toward Whonnock was badly marked on the highway, and, in any case, the grey rain made visibility poor. "I think we've passed the turn," said Ellen.

"I thought you were looking!" ("I was.") "*I* can't see *everything*, can I," said Huw crossly.

That settles it, decided Ellen. The time is set for the drive home. The last thing she wanted was to marry anyone like

Huw Peake and drive about the country with him. There were few foot passengers trudging along in the rain to enquire from, and these walkers in the rain were unintelligent about directions. The general opinion gathered through sheets of rain was that they had passed the turn-up. They backed, turned, and drove along the way they had come, peering. They found the turn-up. There was to be a church at the top of the hill. There were two churches. "What the *hell* . . . " said Huw.

They arrived and saw faces at the streaming window-pane. The door opened on two little people.

"We thought you'd *never* come!" cried Mrs. Ransome. "*Such* a day! You should have *telephoned*! I said to my husband Now shall I put the biscuits in or *not*! So I put them in and I'm afraid they're a teeny bit burnt. So this is Huw! And to think that you were *such* a dear little boy, one of the *dearest* little boys, Miss . . . Miss . . . "

"Cuppy," said Ellen Cuppy.

The dear little boy, tall and scowling, shook hands firmly with Mr. and Mrs. Ransome, who winced. Mr. and Mrs. Ransome were both the same size and looked like elderly twins and were a sidelight to Ellen on Huw's mother. Could anyone ever be insistently fond of Mrs. Ransome, Ellen wondered. She – Huw's mother – is probably one of those women who like everybody, and it is sufficient to have met someone once on a train to incur reciprocal visits and Christmas cards for ever. The conversation was continued on Mrs. Ransome's lines.

"And to think you were a prisoner of war!" she said. "*Tell me*" (confidentially) "how did they treat you? I've often wondered, how *did* they treat you! I used to knit . . . " The prisoner of war looked uncomfortable.

"I'll be frank with you," said Mr. Ransome, gazing upon Huw. "I've never seen a prisoner of war before. You really – if I may say so – look remarkably well. I was in the First War, you know, and there was a fellow in our unit who . . . "

Oh Lord, thought Ellen, prisoner of war *and* the First War! How Huw seems to detest the First War. I can't think why.

"Have you a ranch, Mr. Ransome?" she enquired rudely

and brightly. "Is it mixed farming or what, here? I've always heard that Whonnock . . . " and the conversation continued, tripartite, steered into lines of safe inanity – chickens – churches – biscuits – relatives – peonies – cucumbers – wedding days – and Ellen, getting sillier and sillier, became monumentally aware of Huw, dark and handsome, he and the Prince of Denmark and these tedious old fools, inexcusable, a molten image smoking too many cigarettes. No sane person would mistake him for a happy lover. This was a pleasant afternoon, wasn't it.

"And when is the happy day, did you say?" enquired Mr. Ransome for the second time. Happy day, the old idiot, thought the bridegroom and did not answer.

Ellen smiled sweetly and said, "We haven't settled that yet."

"Ah, you young people! These are happy days, happy days! Make the best . . . enjoy them while you may!"

"And you *will* come again, won't you," urged Mrs. Ransome, "some really *fine* day! The country *so* lovely! And then you will see our peonies! A nice little jaunt in the country . . . now *promise*!"

"Oh in*deed, yes*! It's been a *delightful* afternoon in spite of the rain," said Ellen falsely. (Who are we to be so snooty? Letters, and making biscuits, and two elderly noses at the rainy window-pane, and Huw sitting there with hardly a word forced out of him, and me making a silly of myself.)

"Goodbye! *Good*bye!"

Slam went the car door, and they drove away, neither one speaking for a time.

Life is unfair, thought Ellen. Mr. and Mrs. Ransome are innocent and tiresome and quite old, and devouring, and eager, and Huw and I are snooty and heartless and will ourselves be old some day (how tedious Heaven knows) and Huw has behaved like the very devil and I am a monster of duplicity – both ways. It was plain that Huw was unable to tolerate the fault of tedium in the aged.

As she sat in the car she saw future Saturdays and Sundays. Years and years of them, and Huw who had behaved badly behaving worse with a lifetime of experience, and she – making amends, making amends, until her whole life was a continuous making amends, and apprehension, and duplicity, and the fresh joys of life all gone. She would never be able to look forward without apprehension in case Huw would be in a bad temper; he would probably come home annoyed, bringing his bad temper with him ready for anything that might arise; she would have to adjust herself ceaselessly, and, even then, nothing would be improved thereby; children would make it worse; love (which is said to be enough) would not be enough. She looked sideways at Huw whom – but not at that moment – she loved. Have Mr. and Mrs. Ransome no rights at all? Haven't they even the right to be dull? Must I always play the cackling fool? She was angry, and ready to speak her mind. She began to do so . . .

But Huw said, staring over the wheel, not "Well, *that's* over, darling" but "That's a hell of a way to spend an afternoon! You seemed to enjoy it – all right, all right . . . well, I only said you seemed to anyway . . . You seem to like those kind of people . . . but let me tell you, believe me, when we're married I sincerely hope . . . " The car was full of anger.

It was not hard to break in now and to tell him that nothing would induce her to marry him because she could not endure his bad temper.

"*Me!* Bad-tempered!" said Huw, genuinely surprised. "Just because I can't stick people like that and I can't pretend like you do . . . " He became virtuous and the quarrel went back to front and developed along the wrong lines.

They could not get to the end of the drive fast enough. They both said things that they became sorry for and, later, Ellen felt humiliated. She did not know what Huw really felt. She said at the last as the storm abated, "But can't we be friends, Huw?"

"*Friends!*" he exclaimed, looking at her as though he despised her, and then he drove off, and that was the end of it.

It sounded ridiculous. The engagement was broken because they quarrelled – what about? About old Mr. and Mrs.

Ransome, and the rain, and losing their way, and the knock in the engine. No no no, said Ellen desperately, alone in her room and in tears, it wasn't those things. It was something more, much more.

Morgan was displeased with Ellen's behaviour. Nora said, "But Gypsy, how could you! Have you forgotten that he was a prisoner of war?"

"No," said Ellen very sad for losing Huw, and sad for Huw that he was a prisoner of war and still a prisoner, and glad for losing him, "no, I didn't forget, truly, Nora, I didn't forget."

Let's chalk it up to experience, say the apologists. But next time it's never the same.

So she went to stay for a while with Mary and John Livingstone in Saskatoon where she did not feel herself to be the object of comment and disapproval. I shall never take a chance again, she thought. I shall become, gradually, an old maid just like Miss Sneddon. I have no alternative. I could not endure all that again.

Huw was deeply shocked at the things that Ellen said to him and for a while he cherished a hardness against her whom he had really loved. But his heart was not broken. He found her, in retrospect, desirable but very unreasonable. She had accused him of bad temper when he had simply spoken his mind! If she had only been a little more reasonable, he thought, they could have made a good go of it. He saw too often her small curly head and her bright turning to him as they walked so well together and drove about together. He regretted her until at last she faded away and was forgotten by her lover.

After about the same long space of time the passion of these two was as nothing to either of them although it had been exciting, and enchanting, and then a burden; but sometimes Huw was brought vividly to Ellen's mind by some other person. Then the whole experiment, and the failure, and the break-up came sharply back to her and she fortified herself against the encroachments of love.

Twenty

IN SASKATOON, in spite of the wide Saskatchewan river, Ellen missed the salt water which she had lived beside all her life, but it was no temptation to return to Vancouver where Huw was, and where Morgan – whom she would often see – was still incensed with her on his step-brother's behalf. Morgan had a righteous disapproval of her; he thought she had been wanton and cruel in her treatment of Huw who had been a prisoner for days and nights and weeks and months and years, and deserved patience and support and at least a return of affection. He said little to Nora as he did not wish to upset her, but he was disappointed in Gypsy who had always seemed to be affectionate and intuitive although not demonstrative except in a quick laughing way. Huw seemed more morose than ever, and his older brother – who had more discernment and compassion than one might think – was considerate. But as the year wore on, Morgan became aware that his young brother's moroseness was a fault of temperament with which the experiences of the war might or might not have anything to do. He at last admitted to himself that whoever married Huw – Gypsy or another – would need celestial patience. No doubt Gypsy after her short intense association with Huw had divined this. Morgan began to be almost sorry for her as the months went on and Huw demonstrated his intolerance of the human race – clients, and especially the other people in the office, and family, and friends; but he bore with Huw and did not rebuke him, since he (Huw) had been exposed to strain and trouble far beyond the range of the older man's experience.

One day Huw came into his brother's office, stood uncertainly and frowning beside his desk, and then told Morgan abruptly that he did not like living in Vancouver and had decided to leave.

For a moment Morgan did not speak. He was congenitally a loyal political animal as was his father before him. He was almost unable to admit any flaws in the political party which he represented, to whose advancement and interests he was devoted – nor in his wife, although he was aware that some people are more difficult to get on with than other people, and that included Huw. He pursued his legal profession with dogged force and a clearer, less partisan, vision. He conceded the right of any man to make a fool of himself as long as he did not involve other people. But it is almost impossible to make a fool of oneself without involving other people. He would even concede his younger brother's right to do that, but not beyond a certain point . . . a certain point. He had come to know that Huw was not a good subject for either coercion or persuasion. He therefore accepted his statement without argument, saying, "Then are you going back to Toronto?"

"To Toronto? God, no," said Huw as if shocked. "I know a man in San Francisco."

So Huw went to San Francisco and thence to South America. He was labelled unfortunate, and the members of his family did not see him again. If Ellen, thinking of Huw from time to time, had wished to say "Where is Huw? Tell me what has happened to him," there was no one of whom she could enquire. People began to forget that they had ever thought that Ellen had behaved badly. She was only another episode in Huw's stormy passage. Morgan said to himself regarding himself, Well, I have failed.

John Livingstone, who had married Mary Ford who had been stationed with Ellen in the Haymarket, found a secretary's job for her in Saskatoon with a rich old man named Mr. Platt.

Twenty-One

JOHN LIVINGSTONE, who was Mr. Platt's lawyer, said to Ellen, "Platt is unique in this generation of spenders, he's out of date . . . I bet you my life he sits with his bonds and strokes them . . . greed's okay and avarice is out of fashion, but no, there's always Platt to keep up the good old ways . . . don't be scared. You'll belong to another side of Mr. Platt altogether, he likes a bit of panache, it's the only luxury he allows himself, you and his new front office. You'll be his interior decorator and his adviser, and you'll sit in your office looking beautiful, re-writing his letters and typing them – oh it's all right, I'll protect you . . . I'm the keeper of Platt's conscience, he won't involve you in anything though he's got a genius for evasion and he certainly dislikes the law . . . and you're not to have red finger nails . . ."

"I shall do exactly as I like about that," said Ellen, amused by this new picture of herself as a fine front for Mr. Platt – a change from the Navy.

Every town possesses its unique person who ceases to be a unique person because his behaviour and appearance have become familiar and accepted and he has merged into the colour and decoration of the town as does that old house with wedding-cake trimmings (relic of gentility) near the entrance to the park, or the whiskered bust of the first mayor. If the wedding-cake trimmings were removed from the peculiar house in favour of a chaste façade, or the mayor and his whiskers were replaced by a piece of sculpture symbolic of early settlement but unrecognizable as such, people would be aggrieved as they would be if Mr. Platt should buy and wear an ordinary suit and hat. They would have a right to be aggrieved. When Ellen arrived in Saskatoon she (like other newcomers) was at first surprised at the appearance of Mr. Platt, who had for so long been accepted by the people of the town that he was no longer noticeable to himself nor to anyone else, but she soon became accustomed to him.

Mr. Platt was small, neat and urbane. His outside peculiarity consisted in wearing on his small body a closely fitting black suit, a heavy gold watch chain, and on his small neat head a hat which might be called a square bowler which was sometimes too large and sometimes too small. He carried an umbrella of gamp-like appearance. The suit was always old, and the hat was always new, and the gamp was eternal. Although the suit was black in origin and intention, it was now what is called a suit green with age. Such suits are not green, but have – even the best of them – developed over the years an aura of glancing greenness which justifies the word green. Where did Mr. Platt come from? Nearly everyone in this young city came from somewhere. Nobody knew, and nobody cared at all, so that when at last Mr. Platt died, leaving his wealth behind him but no relatives, or friends, newspaper reporters, becoming very busy, were frustrated, and could discover nothing in the pre-history of Mr. Platt. Someone thought he had been a gentleman's gentleman but no one could prove it. He had arrived in Winnipeg forty years before with a discreet fortune of twenty thousand dollars, and he at that time wore a black suit and an even then obsolete black hat, carried an umbrella and had no relatives. Mr. Platt, still earlier but unrecorded, stepping inquisitively over the great pre-Cambrian Shield, dressed in black and wearing his good square bowler, must have caused disquiet to the original inhabitants, the wolverine and the porcupine, and others, who had seen nothing in those unpeopled wastes to compare with him.

"Why is his suit so old and his hat so new?" asked Ellen of John Livingstone. "Did he buy a job lot?"

"Never buys anything. Creditors' estate. Coupla dozen. Different sizes. Perfectly harmless except in business, then he's lethal."

"And the watch chain? It's like a ship's anchor chain."

"Deceased relative, he told me, and that's the only thing he ever did say . . . about himself, I mean. What could be more respectable than a deceased relative with a watch chain . . . sort of identification with the herd for Platt. I think he cherishes the respectability of the whole get-up . . . I'd call him conservative. How's the interior decorating coming along?"

Mr. Platt stepped unobtrusively into his newly furnished offices as if he were going to ask himself for a loan, and looked about him, a little scared.

"Very nice, Miss Um," he said at last. "I like a bit of Art on the walls myself. That *is* Art, I presume? Myself I prefer a pretty pitcher of a nice young lady with a pleasant smile, clothed *or* classical . . . but you wouldn't think that suitable for an office of this nature? No, perhaps not. If you say that pitcher's Art, I shall believe you, but it doesn't look like Art to me. I shall no doubt become accustomed to it. Them's handsome . . . " he said, fingering the heavy curtains which Ellen had ordered at his expense for the two small but magnificent offices. As he stood and surveyed this scene (his own) joy arose within him, swelled, possessed, and almost shook him. "Get the bills in quick, Miss Um" (before it hurts too much). Mr. Platt called Ellen Miss Um throughout the years that she spent in Saskatoon. She grew almost fond of him – he was so solitary – although she was lordly with him. He preferred it.

"How can you stand him?" asked her friends.

"He's a very interesting person."

"He'll make you his heir."

"Oh no, he won't. I'll see to that."

Instead of her days being empty in this new town, Ellen's days were full. People were friendly. At first, time flew fast. Her father, on his way to potential oil-fields, visited her twice. Once she spent her holidays in New York. His wife Nicola, grown heavier, suited him well. Ellen felt affection for Nicola, but it seemed shocking, at moments, that her mother who had been their source and centre was quite removed from their lives; it was nobody's fault (what becomes of us, with all this living?) but Mother had irrevocably gone, and taken her ambience with her. Not only Mother had gone, but all those who . . . It is, she reflected, only the common lot of ordinary people, of all of us, even of emperors, but something stays, added to the general sum, which is not just memory, and it does not do to mind . . . but she was grateful to Nicola.

Usually, Ellen spent her holiday with Nora. Sometimes Morgan was in Ottawa, sometimes in Vancouver. The house revolved around the cherub who, year by year, crept, toddled, walked, and lived in a climate of adulation, from his mother (lost in her dream), from his nurse, and from his visiting aunt. Ellen returned to Saskatoon each year faintly uneasy on the cherub's behalf.

Twenty-Two

ELLEN LIVED in the upper part of a house on a road which skirted the high bank of the Saskatchewan river. In the summer time her windows looked on to trees, and then on the broad river, and then on the bridge, and then on the far bank of the river where the University stands, built of native field stone of fine varying colour.

In the winter time her windows looked on snow and the cold river, and again on snow enveloping ground, bridge, houses, motor cars, people, University – and sometimes the sky of which there was a great deal. In certain seasons of the year the Northern Lights moved across half the sky, beyond passion, mysterious.

One winter afternoon the telephone rang as she came into her warm flat.

A man's voice said that this was George Gordon from Montreal and that a mutual friend in Montreal by the name of Marcel Lajoie had asked him to telephone her. Ellen had played badminton with Marcel Lajoie when he lived in Saskatoon. In fact she was playing in the semi-finals that very evening at the badminton club, and when George Gordon told her that he used to play badminton with Marcel Lajoie and asked her to have dinner with him at the hotel, Ellen told him that she would like to do this but would have to have dinner very early, and would he feel inclined to go on with her to badminton, and he said he would.

They had dinner together and went to the badminton club.

Ellen was beaten in the semi-finals, and George Gordon was not at all bored as he had expected to be that first evening in Saskatoon. He had only telephoned Ellen as an escape from dining en famille with the company director whom he had come to see and with whom he would spend the next day and a half. He at once asked Ellen to dine with him the next night, which she did.

Twenty-Three

INSTEAD OF becoming more sociable when his marriage had broken up, instead of seeking his friends and entertainment, George Gordon had withdrawn into himself and had become solitary. He diverted his energies into business and – later – into books.

When his marriage failed he discovered a vulnerable pride within himself of which he was not aware, for how can a man know himself until the unexpected worst arrives? When everything was over and his wife Maidie had moved on with her usual vivacity to another marriage as soon as possible, George Gordon found that the hurt to his pride was disproportionate and constant; he woke with it in the morning and it met him everywhere. What! He and Maidie had lived together in short intervals of the war and in the years following the war. They had slept together and woken together night after night and morning after morning – all the intimacy of marriage, and then came the niggling dissensions, the boredom, the deceptions of the enraging Maidie, the discoveries, the infidelity and Maidie shockingly up to her tricks and there was no more cajoling that had been so pretty and then so silly, and then so irritating. The intolerable hurt to his pride did not prevent his losing himself in business, although in the company of other men with women he felt stripped. I'm a fool, he said, to take it like this . . . it happens to plenty of people . . . (look at Angus, and . . .) it's egotism, just cheap egotism. When he said, "I'm sorry, I have a Hospital Board meeting that night", or "No I can't, I have some men in town from New York that I have to look after", and when he went home to his flat and at last took down a book from his shelves or opened some of the papers and reviews that began to pile up on his desk, and read into the evening and into the night, he knew that this was more congenial than evening company. A kind of steadying began at last within him. The evenings gradually became endurable but this was not really his life.

"Poor old George," said Maidie who had a pretty little nose and no tiresome inhibitions and had been his wife, "everyone says no one ever sees him anywhere. It's absurd his acting in this broken-hearted way," she said rather pleased. "Look!" she said virtuously, "you and I might have acted like that but what'd be the good of it to anybody! He should find some girl, don't you think so, Tommy, don't you really think so? They say he's turning into a bookworm! George a bookworm!" and she laughed merrily, and Tommy her husband who had not been interested in George Gordon for some time past thought, Women certainly haven't much sense, Maidie hasn't much sense, and said, "Well, cheerio."

When George had occasion to pay his first visit to Saskatoon en route to the coast he knew that he would spend most of his time with a J.B. Honeybee whom he had already met, and with Mr. Honeybee's associates. Enough is enough, he said to himself, and on his arrival in a strange town as remote almost as the Pole, he thought to steer himself into one evening's variety, and into two evenings if he liked this friend of Marcel's, this Ellen Cuppy. Then he would not be glued to J.B. Honeybee for two days nor J.B. Honeybee to him. He was not looking for entertainment – he did not even feel sociable although more emancipated than in Montreal. He was seeking only for "a previous engagement", a means of escape, and what happened to him was that he found himself, later in the evening, in the old familiar sound and sight, quick movement and play of a badminton tournament. No one knew that he was George Gordon whose wife Maidie had left him ingeniously and light-heartedly and at much expense and trouble to all concerned; no one cared whether he was single, married, divorced, a recluse, or the victim of pride; and no one said "Poor George". Everyone was playing or watching the badminton. Someone lent him a pair of shoes and he had a game of mixed doubles on the far court when things were over. So quick the game was again, a little too quick now. For his part, the last thing he desired was to become involved with any girl however nice she seemed, but it was pleasant to be in badminton again after so long, and the game wiped out the usual evening awareness and staleness, for that night at least. Next day he was surprised and a little shocked to feel stiff.

The following year George Gordon came again to Saskatoon en route to the coast. He wrote to Ellen ahead of time so as not to miss the pleasure of seeing her. One evening he told her, awkwardly, of his marriage. I thought, said Ellen to herself, there was something like that. I am sorry for him; she must be crazy or – well, who can tell. He is nice. Ellen had other things upon her mind at that time; but, later, the monitor within gave warning and also gave the peculiar pleasure that usually accompanies the warning, that disturbance that murmurs Fire Fire.

Twenty-Four

ELLEN CONTINUED living on the prairies; Nora, in Vancouver, watched her little son growing; Frank Cuppy, in New York, came and went, but not so often now and not so far. He was three thousand miles nearer his heart of things, and three thousand miles and return may not be far as the plane flies but it is not negligible. Morgan Peake, living on a periphery, flew his three thousand miles several times a year, which is sometimes one part of living in the West. The traveller, travelling and retravelling his three thousand miles, dozes, reads, ignores the scene (as Morgan does, now), or finds his mind full of amazement and speculation.

No picture can show how wide the country is; no map convey. Once traversing will not do. Each time the uninterested traveller crosses the Dominion of Canada by the northern route, by the southern route, or by air, the journey becomes more intolerably long, the forests more intolerably endless, the prairies are more boringly monotonous, the lakes interminable, the mountains monstrous, until the Pacific Ocean is reached. Each time the interested traveller crosses the country by the northern route, by the southern route or by air, the country with its sleeping past, its awakened future, the gradual progress of discovery and habitation, the extravagant forests, prairies, lakes, and mountains, the great beauty, the isolated and sometimes collapsed shack that speaks of human effort and departure, the sudden appearance of a city in all that solitude (like an explosion) – the land enchants and speaks to him. The land is full of question. The journey disturbs and exhilarates. The traveller – be he interested or bored by size and continuity, by history or non-history – begins his journey in Ontario, in Quebec, or the eastern seaboard. When he has travelled to the far confines of British Columbia he returns, like George Gordon, to his home. He has made his journey. He may return to the West, but perhaps he does not return, for there are other places in the world to see. It is a long way to go.

But the dweller in the West has made his journey not very long ago, not much more than a century ago, or yesterday – he or his English father, his Scottish great-grandfather, his Irish uncle, his European parents, his grandparents from Upper or Lower Canada, his American forebears, or the Welshman Morgan Peake – each has reached the shores that the English captain had already charted and named for him. He does not show a disposition to rest. The same disposition that brought Captain George Vancouver to the coast and brought these newcomers westward keeps them or their descendants on the move. They will not so often travel further westward now – there is nothing but the Pacific Ocean to move into, and the lands beyond, already pre-empted and foreclosed, but they may turn to the North. This newcomer and his sons and daughters who live on a periphery and are animated by circumstance and the urge that brought them there and by the fact that there is somewhere a place that remains (as yet) a centre, are moved by these things to go across the country again and again (as soon as they can afford it, or before) to this centre wherever it may be, to do their business there or to refresh themselves there with the things that a periphery cannot provide. They then return across this country, content, to their homes. They are content only for a time, and then the same disposition for movement creeps up and seizes them again. They go vast distances over the North Pole to Britain, they go by freighter to Portugal, they go to New York by train, they motor to California, they fly to Quebec and the Maritime Provinces. They are not confined by their distance. They go.

It follows, with all this going, that the eastern, populous part of their country is familiar to them. The fact that these western people live on a periphery tempts them continually to move and return, move and return, very like birds. But they return.

So, for every mile travelled by his fellow Members of Parliament, Morgan Peake and his western colleagues travelled many miles, taking the journey for granted. So did Morgan's wife Nora in the days before Johnny was born; so did her father in the years when his home – and Susan's – was in Vancouver. (Canada is much too big, Susan used to affirm.) The almost alarming spaciousness of the land exacts this. The formidable power of geography determines the character and performance of a people; it invokes understanding or prejudice; it makes peace or war. A land that stretches across a continent extends in breadth and in some homogeneity; it gives flattering promise of peace; but in a land which is crushed in the middle of Europe or Asia, anxieties are renewed. It is the fault of geography.

"And is Morgan back from Ottawa?" asked Morgan's old cousin Miss Sneddon, leaning forward with aged earnestness.

"Yes, he came back on Monday, but he thinks he'll have to fly back for a meeting next week," said Nora.

"Dear, dear," said little Miss Sneddon politely, thinking not of a periphery but of how, really and truly, Morgan was getting to be as much of a traveller as poor Susan's husband used to be. And now Ellen Cuppy coming and going like this and the papers full of people travelling. . . . all these people . . . . flying flying. . . . thinking nothing of flying across Canada and back, and across the ocean, just like a street-car ride I do declare . . . (when I remember . . .)

Nora was speaking, checking a flood. "Wouldn't you like to see Johnny?" she asked, smiling, serene, promising something.

Twenty-Five

"WELL, MAKE up your mind," said John Livingstone genially and brutally to Mr. Platt. "Next thing you'll be found dead in your bed and no will." Mr. Platt continued a fit of coughing.

"I've neether chick nor child," he said at last. He did not wish for either, nor did he want a will. He liked saying that he had neither chick nor child, and in the solitude of his bedroom at the top of a cheap hotel he would murmur with satisfaction, "I've neether chick nor child", and he enjoyed the bargain-price luxury of a specious sorrow for a lonely old man who was not in the least lonely.

"Mr. Livingstone spoke to me again about getting to work on your will," said Ellen later to Mr. Platt. "I've drawn up a list of your assets as far as I can, but it's not complete. If you will give me the whole list, we'll go ahead."

"I've neether chick . . . "

"I know, no chickens and no children. If you really want chickens I'll get you some. If you want young children the Children's Aid needs funds and if you want old children the University needs scholarships."

"You and Mr. Livingstone don't know what it is to be a lonely old man," mumbled Mr. Platt evasively.

"Yes we do," said Ellen.

Ellen was well aware that if she should urge the needs of any part of the human race, local, national, or global, Mr. Platt would retreat at once from making his will. He could not bear that anyone else should possess, even potentially, even on paper and certainly not in expectation, the common and preferred stocks, the bonds, the oil holdings, the leaseholds, the winery, the linoleum factory, that traction company in South America that made him so nervous. Ellen neither suggested nor urged, but she said with an indulgent look that Mr. Platt evaded, "Even I have made a will, and I'm not as old as you are nor as rich."

"Very nice, Miss Um, very nice. We're all of us yuman and no one can't escape the Grim Reaper . . . I've no use for real estate what with maintenance and depreciation and repairs but there's a sweet tempting little proposition in Winnipeg that I'm thinking of getting for quick re-sale. It come my way. There's the particulars, you get Mr. Livingstone to draw up the papers . . . "

He would swallow still another investment, satisfied as a heron is satisfied with one more fish in its gullet. Death, as the Grim Reaper, was a rhetorical shade. Some curious unrealistic inversion made Mr. Platt refuse to admit the immediacy of death because it was so close. Just as, perhaps, Ellen herself – almost aware of a sameness, a less-brightness, near at hand – refused to acknowledge this less-brightness into which she had begun to move. Friendship and sports were still her preoccupations, but more often lately she had thought, I will leave Mr. Platt. I have finished here. Where shall I go? To the sea again.

Now, when the easy useless working day was done, she attended evening classes at the University. After the lectures were ended, the students, old and young, issuing by twos and threes, stood in groups, talking talking under the great prairie sky of evening. The sky of the prairie is enormous. Light lasts on in the northland, and against the still luminous great sky of night the small groups of people of all ages stood outlined, and then gradually dispersed. Many students were of foreign birth and some came from distant farms and isolated small communities sharing the same prairies, the same sky, the same iron cold and summer heat, the same kind of solitude and toil, gathered together here for a time. Ellen and her friends were younger than many of these evening students, older than others, but now she felt older than all of them. She had begun to be teased sometimes by the discrepancy between the trivia of life and its purposes. Unexpected results came from insignificant happenings; significant moments brought revelation; history and time and change disclosed these things. She was restless but not unhappy.

After the long voyage, years ago, the young Ellen (who was still Gypsy) had flown home and had found herself, wherever she looked, alone. Mother, who had so sweetly composed and pervaded her life, was gone. Her outer life easily conformed; she was gregarious and never solitary; but her inner life became question and answer, question and no answer. She was chary of opening her mind to anyone, and with bright ardent eyes she looked around her. Nora was still the absently dutiful sister because Susan had gone ("Gypsy, I think you ought to . . . "). Ellen's inner non-conformity did not seriously separate the sisters. Simply, within herself, Ellen did not conform, and that habit of mind continued.

When the girls were little, or at least when Ellen was very young, Susan's purest and most private pleasure used to come at the end of the day when a child knelt by her knees saying "Our Father Which Art in Heaven". The pale golden Nora said her prayers politely. She went to bed and fell asleep at once, but with Ellen there was always controversy.

Kneeling there, Ellen would continue to argue stiffly.

"But grown-ups don't have troubles?"

"Why not?"

"Because they're grown-up."

"Oh yes they do. Sometimes they have little tiny troubles like those aggravating women whispering in the strings movement last night or bigger ones like that week when we lost Tiger – or big ones like when Daddy went away with that cough and temperature – and lots of grown-ups have awful troubles, Gypsy, like no homes and no friends and no food, or if I'd run over that little boy today, *that's* a trouble for a grown-up . . . "

"Well, why don't they pray?"

"A lot of them do. Praying won't always take trouble away but it makes it easier for you and me to understand and manage. Prayer's like a cup, Gypsy, sent full of blessings from God."

"The King doesn't have troubles, though?"

"Yes, he does, God save him, because he's a man as well as a King. He has both kinds."

"And does he have to pray, too?"

"Yes, I think he prays every day and that helps him to be a good man, and you see, Gypsy, it makes us all one family. The prayer doesn't say 'Give *me* this day *my* daily bread', it says 'Give *us* *our* daily bread' . . . and that means all of us. Come, now."

Then Gypsy would screw up her eyes in the way prescribed for prayer, and for some time, when she was very small, Susan let her continue to say, "Harold be Thy Name." In the evening it was a delicious pleasure for her to hear the innocent words.

Prayer was a legacy that Susan left to her younger daughter. Sometimes, as years moved on, the words of prayer seemed vain. But more often prayer was to Ellen as though the windows and doors of her spirit were opened wide. Susan died before age exacted from her the necessary graces of age – patience, good temper, and gratitude; but she had all these within her for bestowal, and more than these.

Twenty-Six

GEORGE GORDON arrived at Saskatoon on his way to the coast and stopped there again on his return journey. This time he and Ellen skated. The mere passage of time, even without association, had established a rapport between them. Ellen had become increasingly important to him, and, because she was important to him, he thought he knew her well. He is one of the nice things that happen to me, Ellen thought. She was aware of his qualities; she heard them in his voice and saw them in his face. Yet she did not know him. His appearance pleased and then charmed her but he was by no means necessary to her. She was not so young now, that she should imagine or require perfection. Rather, it was in her nature to be sceptical of perfection. Yet when he asked her to marry him (as she at last knew he would) her liking for him did not prevent Huw arising uninvoked, and at once her freedom became essential to her again. This free life-without-an-object, which had become so boring, was suddenly necessary to her security. She knew this life well, and would not exchange it for some other life which might be only a new conformity, and then perhaps a prison far away with a stranger.

"I don't know you well enough, George," she said, her candid brown eyes wide open and the lashes fringed back. "You don't know me either, but that's not the only reason . . ." and then came the threadbare words, "I like you so much but I don't love you . . . no, or I couldn't bear you going off again like this . . . it would be no good," she said, looking at him honestly.

He considered for a moment.

"Very well. That's your decision. Let's forget it." He was so easy and agreeable that she was a little frightened. She had expected persuasion, and was not sure that she had not been lightly slapped.

George said at the airport, "I won't forget to send you Samuel Butler. I think you'll like him." George was not the hurt and rejected one, meet for sympathy, and Ellen was not the rejector. They said goodbye.

Flying above the prairies George considered his lack of persistence. Perhaps his tactics were good. It's hard to know what's wise, he thought, but at least Ellen is Ellen and different from other people, and that's the way I must play it. The plane tore the clouds apart and the clouds closed behind again without a mark. The passengers gazed with vacant looks upon the air. Then they settled to sleep uncomfortably, or they read. George turned from the clouds to the stock market and again to Ellen Cuppy whom he intended to marry.

Twenty-Seven

FROM *Samuel Butler's Note-Books*. Typed by George Gordon's secretary in Montreal.

"The Corpse's Brother.

"At a funeral the undertaker came up to a man and said to him, 'If you please, Sir, the corpse's brother would be happy to take a glass of sherry with you.'"

"New Languages.

"English will be the universal language, but each profession will, by and by, come to have a subordinate dialect of its own which will be hardly understood by those of another profession. The longer we can delay this the better."

"Aimez-vous donc les Beautés de la Nature?

"A man told me that at some Swiss hotel he had been speaking enthusiastically about the beauty of the scenery and a Frenchman said to him: 'Aimez-vous donc les beautés de la nature? Pour moi je les abhorre.'"

"Death is only a larger kind of going abroad."

George Gordon said to Ellen in his letter, "Here are the bits I typed for you and they will show you what *Samuel Butler's Note-Books* are like. You shall have a copy as soon as I can get a good one. I'm sending you a pile of books shortly. You don't have to read them."

Ellen said to herself, He is one of the nicest people in the world but I don't want to be controlled by him or by anybody, books or no. A shade behind a shade said, Take care . . . this may not come your way again.

Twenty-Eight

IT IS POSSIBLE that a relation exists between the reading habits of a nation and its climate. England is, relatively, a nation of readers and uncertain weather. Umbrellas abound, and mists, and twilights, and four – sometimes cold – enclosing walls with a door, as a retreat; the "ranch house" (with or without ranch) has not yet imposed its bland publicity, within and without. In the brilliant superficiality of light as it falls on the prairies – light on the white of the usable snow, on the far-spread, expectant green or yellow of crops, on the naked brown of fallow, in the aurora borealis of half the sky which demands the whole attention – Ellen and her friends were not greatly concerned with reading ("some day I really mean to read"), which is a secluded affair; yet the reader is never solitary.

"Do you like reading?" George Gordon had asked, curiously.

"Reading? Yes, I do," said Ellen who thought she did.

"I'll send you some things some time," he had said, and now the books had arrived. In the accompanying letter he did not mention other matters, which pleased her, or was she a little dismayed.

When Ellen went to Vancouver for her last summer's holiday from the prairies she was recalled by John Livingstone because one morning early a night watchman saw a light in Mr. Platt's office in the Platt Investment Building. It was both too early and too late for a light.

The watchman, whose name was Mac, made his way into the office. He had some difficulty in unlocking the inner door. When he succeeded in opening the door he stood and looked at the small aged body of Mr. Platt which lay upon the desk. Documents covered the desk in what had been orderly piles until they were disarranged by the sudden death of Mr. Platt. His head now rested suitably upon his darlings, and his hat lay upon the floor.

"Gosh," said the night watchman. After looking carefully at Mr. Platt, he took up the telephone.

Ellen returned at once to Saskatoon and worked with John Livingstone to set Mr. Platt's affairs in order. The facts that he had not made a will, that he was without relatives, and that he was secretive added to the difficulties. The weather was hot. When a certain point was reached, John Livingstone advised Ellen to go back to the coast for two weeks' rest and cool weather and then return to help him wind up affairs. Although forgotten as a human being, Mr. Platt remained for some time a legal nuisance.

This event prompted George Gordon to write again to Ellen, demonstrating to her that it was absurd that she should continue not to marry him. He nearly wrote "especially now that you're out of a job", but refrained, as she might not think that funny. He then abandoned his usual casual manner of writing and told her again that he loved her, ending "I want you here my dearest Ellen. Couldn't you be happy here?"

John Livingstone, who fancied himself an artist, took a caustic delight in the manner of Mr. Platt's death, which was not unexpected. Appropriate Platt, he thought sententiously; how rarely do life and art combine in such perfection, such pleasing suitability.

PART THREE

A Scar

Twenty-Nine

A SEAGULL cried in a strange voice outside the window Gedunk – gedunk – gedunk and then went off into a harsh chattering frenzy. Inside the room no one seemed to notice. There were always seagulls.

Three people were in the room, not to speak of their ancestors. The little fair boy lay upon his stomach on the floor and spilt paint water on the carpet. His fair mother, who had once been ethereal and was now handsome, leaned back with her hands resting lightly on the arms of her chair. She watched the child with sleepy indulgence and seemed lost in the miracle of her son, painting, and spilling water on the carpet.

The third person in the room was the younger sister of this mother. This was Ellen Cuppy. While her older sister, Mrs. Morgan Peake, lay back and watched her son, Miss Cuppy leaned against the mantelpiece, sometimes shifting her position. She was tall, and slight, and might be athletic, and in fact she was. She looked about twenty-six or twenty-seven. She was a dark young woman, with a short face and bright brown eyes. The hair on her good little head was dark and strong, and curled upwards like brown feathers. She was dressed in a grey skirt and sweater, and round her neck she wore a red silk handkerchief. If it had not been for the red silk handkerchief you would not think at once (as you did) of a gypsy; and that look was why she had been called in her family since her childhood, Gypsy or Gyp.

The two sisters were, in essence, unlike. While Mrs. Peake reclined placidly unaware of anything but her small son – unaware above all of herself – Ellen was very much aware, and her bright dark look ranged about the room, resting on the small boy, and upon her sister. The child looked up. He held his brush suspended.

"And the house is pink, and the children are going to be blue . . . "

"You see," said his mother, smiling fondly, " . . . modern . . . these things come so naturally to children . . . the child mind . . . they have no doubts . . . they must be right . . . "

"Must they?" said Ellen and walked across the room to the window.

The window overlooked False Creek, which fulfils its name by not being a creek but being a small arm of the sea, terminating very briefly; so that one wonders how it can contain the innumerable tugs, fishing boats, booms of logs, scows, barges, dredges, and even small oil tankers which enter the creek and are moored beside its limited shores.

Ellen saw from the window that the tide was unusually high, and was running in swiftly and with a fresh wind, so that False Creek appeared to be a river running strongly in the wrong direction. Out of the widening mouth of the creek came a medium-sized and handsome tug pulling two barges. Ellen detached herself from whatever it was that irritated her as she had stood in the room looking at her sister and her nephew, and became lost immediately in the extreme beauty of the tug and the way in which the tug rose and fell as it breasted and pushed forward against the running grey sea that opposed it.

When Ellen visited her sister Nora Peake, she was sometimes disturbed in her thoughts. She even became bored and frequently turned her attention to the tugs that ply up and down the channel of False Creek. Each tug, large or small, high at the bow, low at the stern, has a proud bearing, and has, indeed, a noble line and small dignity possessed by no other ship afloat. The tugs in this creek do not fuss around the high walls of large vessels, pushing and pulling; they proceed with gallant bearing up or down the channel, beginning or ending the tow's journey, or going on the way up the coast perhaps or to Vancouver Island, on the errand of picking up another tow and pulling it across the Gulf of Georgia in face of whatever weather there may be. There is, Ellen thought, something corporate about a tug when looked at from this height and distance. There were men, of course, on this small boat which she watched rising and dipping, with the seas parting white at its mouth and the two empty scows following biddably behind; but one could also imagine the tug itself as sentient, and, of itself, choosing and functioning. The tug bowed and rose and bowed again.

"What is that piece of rough masonry offshore with the broken pillar sticking out of the base, even at high tide?" asked Ellen.

"I don't know. I've wondered," said Nora not turning her head.

". . . even at the base of Pompey's statua," (which all the while ran blood) murmured Ellen.

"Pompey's what?" asked her sister.

"Oh nothing. Statua."

On the base of Pompey's statua a cormorant sat. Its neck was long, a twisted periscope, a snake. She watched the black flight of another cormorant which settled on the low base of the statua, rose up, spread heraldic wings, subsided again, and spread the wings again, holding them for some time outspread and motionless. She thought about cormorants (strange birds); they are ugly and they are peculiarly beautiful . . . they sit without speaking, unlike gulls . . . do cormorants utter a word? . . . do they walk? . . . they do not sit on the top of the pillar as gulls do, but always low, on the base . . . why do they spread their wings like that, look, again . . . I once counted forty-five . . . she continued to herself.

"Teatime now, wash handies," said her sister briskly, and Ellen turned and saw the child dip and wash his paint brush, suck it thoughtfully and scramble to his feet. There were streaks of paint on his face. "Who is Mummy's dirty little hero?" asked his mother, smiling.

The child did not answer.

"Who is Mummy's dirty little hero?" she repeated more loudly.

"Johnny," said the little boy and trotted out of the room.

Ellen threw herself into a chair. She sat with awkward grace and scowled at her sister.

"Johnny simply adores painting," said Nora. "Did you notice . . . he has a remarkable eye for colour."

"Has he?" said his aunt. All our lives I did not ever think there'd be anything in the world – anything within reason – that I could not talk about to Nora if I had to, fight with her even if necessary; but here it is. When it's your child, everything is different. And so she sat scowling.

Then, "Does Johnny have any boys to play with?" she asked abruptly.

"He has a party, and we *did* have the Abbott boys twice, but something seemed to go wrong. I didn't like to ask and of course Johnny's such a little man he wouldn't tell, so I haven't invited them again."

"I've been thinking," Ellen said, scrutinizing the end of her thumb earnestly, "that I'd like to give Johnny a dog for his birthday – if you'd like him to have one, of course."

" . . . a dog . . . " said Nora.

"I went to Gervin's Kennels and saw a Labrador. He was a darling . . . and they're nice with children . . . "

" . . . oh . . . yes."

"Or there was a spaniel if you like a smaller dog . . . a bitch . . . "

"Do you mind," said Nora looking at the door, "not saying things like that. I don't want Johnny . . . "

" . . . like what . . . " said Ellen Cuppy.

" . . . like what you called the dog."

"All right," said Ellen, sweetly and disagreeably, "all right, Nora, I won't say bitch to Johnny, I'll just say bitch to you" (she hurried on) " . . . but it was a nice little thing, a golden cocker, good with children too."

" . . . a dog," murmured Nora, "I don't really think a dog . . . "

"Or a cat," her sister continued, " . . . a Siamese perhaps."

"Cats have fleas, and they say they sleep on their faces . . . no, not a cat, I *think*. And darling, perhaps I should say it *now* . . . ever since you came out of the Wrens, oh ages and ages ago, but I didn't like to speak then, you use words . . . I mean there's no need to say damn, and some other quite coarse things you say. It's becoming a habit. You don't *mind* my saying this, Gypsy, do you?"

"So!" said Ellen Cuppy. "So I'm coarse" (Nora . . . is it possible . . . can you be saying this . . . today . . . now . . . you must be going nuts) – "well, my dear, it was a coarse war."

"But the war's over long ago," said Nora Peake kindly.

"You think the war's over! I'm glad you think so," said her disagreeable sister, "and," she exploded, "what's more I am not coarse!" (Walking again in St. James's Park with Alan Brown who was soon to be shot down, and seeing and hearing – aghast – the buzz-bomb ride, land and demolish the Guards' Chapel, and the Guards within the Chapel. War's coarse! That's funny!)

Ellen jumped up out of the chair and went to the window again. There were no tugs. "By the way," she said, "while I think of it, I heard from Nicola."

"How's Father?"

"Better."

"Good."

Ellen stood looking at the empty channel and turned as Nora said mildly as though continuing the conversation, "I told you, didn't I, that Morgan's cousin Maud is dead."

"Dead! When?"

"Oh, it must be four or five weeks ago. It was really dreadful. I thought I told you. I was having that huge tea to end all teas that I was telling you about and that very morning about noon her friend Miss McMinn telephoned and told me she was dying. What *could* I do! The telephone going like mad, and "*May* I bring my two cousins" . . . *you* know, but I just had to telephone Mary Morris and tell her to carry on. I *did* wish you were here, Gypsy . . . why do you insist on living in Saskatoon . . . and when I got there it was quite true. She was dying. And I couldn't help the awful feeling of Oh if only

Cousin Maud had died tomorrow instead of today when I could have done so much more, if you know what I mean. Morgan arranged the funeral and it was *very* nice, several wreaths. The Dean and the two old Miss McMinns and Mrs. Vinson – I'd never seen them before, 'the McMinn girls' sixty and seventy at least. Well . . . the poor old thing . . . I thought I'd told you."

So old Miss Sneddon was dead, and had been news, and in the papers. However humble or queer we are, thought Ellen, we're all news once, on our great day, and in the papers. How Miss Sneddon would have enjoyed the paragraph in the Press ("I see in the Press," said Miss Sneddon) and the funeral, and the flowers, with the Dean and the McMinn girls and old Mrs. Vinson, and Morgan and Nora looking so nice ("a tribute I'm sure"). Last time that little Miss Sneddon had tripped smiling in her most fashionable manner into her cousin's house – always on the inconvenient wrong day – and Ellen had been there, she had adjusted herself and had become receptive to old Miss Sneddon, wishing strongly that she – Ellen – had run in from Aunt Maury's yesterday or tomorrow; for however much she and Nora might look forward to an afternoon of easy silences or the give-and-take of talk, no sooner did old Miss Sneddon appear than the situation moved out of their hands. They no longer dominated their air but became the horse on which little Miss Sneddon would – and did – ride. "The only thing," Nora would say afterwards, "is that you don't have to listen. I just shut myself up and let her talk. I never listen."

"But I can't do that," said her sister. "I simply can't not listen. I listen and listen about the McMinn girls until it nearly kills me. But I listen."

"I know, you pay altogether too much attention to people," said Nora, stretching her arms lazily and smiling her sideways Etruscan smile.

"Yes I do," said Ellen.

As those afternoons wore along to the timeless endless ripple of Miss Sneddon's commentary, and after the release of her departure, Ellen sometimes felt uneasy hauntings of the spirit, vague and possible premonitions of age that might find someone else alone some day, trivial, boring, not very welcome...

"Oh, I must go!" Miss Sneddon had said on that last time that Ellen had seen her at Nora's house. "Look! See! It's raining! Dear me, and I never brought my rubbers! I *said* to myself now should I take my rubbers or *shouldn't* I take my rubbers, for the simple reason that last time I took my rubbers it turned out fine and I left them at Mrs. Vinson's sister's. Oh dear me, just look at it, it's coming down in *sheets*! A regular storm to be sure! And so dark all of a sudden! It's a mercy I brought my umbrella and a good thing I got it back from Mrs. Vinson's last Thursday for the simple reason I'd lent it to her because she'd lost hers that her niece gave her and never found it. Well, Nora, it's been *such* a nice visit and Miss Cuppy here! Oh, look at the rain...!"

"Cousin Maud," Nora had said, looking at the rain – they all stood and looked at the rain – "you mustn't go in all this! You must stay to dinner and Morgan will take you home after, he'd love to take you... he has a meeting in town. Take off your hat now..."

"Oh no, that's very good of you I'm sure, Nora, but I simply couldn't" (firmly). "It's Wednesday, and on Wednesday I always have supper with the McMinn girls or they come to me – alternately you know, and I couldn't disappoint them... I don't know what they'd think if I threw them over, for the simple reason we always have a bit of something extra tasty and them taking all that trouble... oh, it's *very* good of you, Nora..." and on and on, the intrepid tiresome little thing.

"Cousin Maud," said Nora, almost crossly, "telephone your friends, *they*'ll understand on a night like this, and Morgan will take you there *directly* after dinner, and you can spend the evening..."

"Oh, I couldn't disappoint the McMinn girls, it's nothing, it's nothing, it will pass... I must go at once."

The very air of the room said Isn't Cousin Maud aggravating! and Ellen pulled on her coat and said, "Come, Miss

Sneddon, I'll run you there, I was going to anyway, wherever it is . . . no, gladly, I assure you, no, I'd like the air" (air indeed), "no, I'll be back in time," and after a good deal of explaining there they were in Ellen's little car, driving through the descending dark and the slanting rain, and on through the shining reflected street lights they went, Miss Sneddon talking talking and Ellen driving. So the last memory she had of Miss Sneddon was of a small figure, very much alive, shining with rain, simultaneously ringing a door-bell and nodding and waving vivaciously at the almost invisible car of that nice Miss Cuppy who always seemed so interested; and now she was dead. My God, Ellen had thought as she drove back to Morgan's in the dark, could I ever some time (standing shrunken a little, at the door) shall I be old Miss Cuppy and Johnny being kind to me . . .

But now, today, she was Ellen Cuppy, young and strong and graceful, with thoughts in her head about George Gordon, and therefore she had no such ideas. "Poor little thing," she said, "I'm sure she arrived in Heaven on the wrong day."

Five years ago, after the unfortunate business of being engaged to Huw, Ellen had been wise to go to her friends in Saskatoon. When from time to time she came back to the coast for her holidays and stayed with her sister and brother-in-law or with other friends, the sisters greeted each other with affection, but now when seven or ten days were gone, the older sister said to her husband when they were going to bed that it was a pity how short-tempered and perverse Gypsy was getting; and she supposed it was not being married, but (she said) there was this man George Gordon who was coming from Montreal and was going to drive with her up to Naramata and it seemed a funny thing to do if she wasn't going to marry him, and Morgan Peake said Yes. Especially now that old Mr. Platt has died, and Morgan, thinking of other things, said Yes.

Nora brushed her hair a while and then she resumed.

"She seems to think I'm making a sissy of Johnny. I said 'Now tell me straight, Gypsy, do you think I'm a possessive mother?' and she said 'Certainly not. But I do think you're making him into a sissy.' She has 'sissy' on the brain. I ask you, Morgan, and Johnny only six!"

"Seven," said Morgan.

"No, strictly speaking *six*," said his wife.

Nora Peake said these family and household things while she put some steel objects into her fair hair until she looked like a modified goddess of Liberty – meet to be admired but not to be fondled.

Mr. Peake responded briefly, and when his striped pyjamas were on he went to the bathroom. He then put his head in at the bedroom door and said to his wife, who was settling, "Well, good night, dolling", and she said "Oh, good night", and their day was done.

Ellen turned with pleasure to the thought of seeing George. They would drive to Isa Cheney's in the Okanagan. They would have an amusing time. Then he would fly home to Montreal. She would spend a pleasant sunny visit with Isa and Charles and the children and then, soothed, smoothed, and renewed, she would come back to Vancouver and say goodbye to Nora and Johnny with great affection (I can do nothing, no, I can do nothing) and with adequate affection to Morgan. Then she would return to Saskatoon and she would marry George as soon as he wished, very quietly, without all this nonsense of a big wedding. Except for her surface irritation with Nora about Johnny becoming a sissy, Ellen was reasonably happy. It was, no doubt, because she had lived on the prairies for the last few years that she felt a strong old affection for the ocean, and for the tugs that plied up and down False Creek, and for the cormorants, even. That was one of the important things whenever she stayed with Mr. and Mrs. Morgan Peake, and was to her a very personal pleasure.

This was the general run of thought that floated through the house, and sometimes small disagreeablenesses were generated. Ellen admonished herself from time to time. For example, she would admit that while she was Johnny's aunt, and thought that he should have a dog, Nora was Johnny's mother, and it might be her little son – so dearly bought and paid for – who would run out into the road after his dog, or her little son who might become infected by the cat who is reputed to sleep on a child's soft face, and not Ellen's nephew. As for Morgan, in spite of knowing him for years, he was really unknown to his wife's clever sister. Knowing people by sight is not enough.

Thirty

NOW, STANDING alone on Mr. and Mrs. Morgan Peake's balcony on a fine fresh morning, leaning upon the rail, Ellen looked down at the water of False Creek flowing out with the tide to mingle with the water of English Bay.

Hundreds of small nameless ducks flowed slowly together in procession on the outgoing tide, replete after a morning's diving and feeding; they flowed and, suddenly, informed with one spirit of motion they all turned sharply against the tide (why? who conferred?), each with its sparkling riffle behind it, making a dazzle of water, and proceeded vigorously upstream in one long line, mysteriously deploying as one against the current, by-passing some mallards, by-passing a cormorant; the mallards, indifferent to the long line of little ducks with their wake of following glitter, came ashore, waddled with clumsy majesty and settled down to sleep instantly on the green grass; the very large cormorant, standing alone on a deadhead, extended its wings and held them motionless, heraldic; tugs issued from False Creek, and . . . if I live to be two hundred, thought Ellen, looking down from the balcony, exulting, I shall never tire of these water matters, seen from this nearness and height; it's life, and more than ordinary life and motion; I cannot explain it because I am not bird or water.

The simple scene conveyed to her that although by her humanity she was excluded, she was a part of these things.

She turned, then, to go into the house. The bright feeling from another place remained for a while with her as she went to the telephone and made complicated arrangements with a dentist, a hairdresser, and three friends who could not play tennis at the same place at the same time. She then found her nephew Johnny and took him, as arranged, to the circus, which they both enjoyed very much. The birds and the water and the small boats were of another kind of enjoyment and were forgotten until the time when Ellen next looked down in leisure upon them.

Thirty-One

MORGAN PEAKE (who was on the brink of becoming a Senator), driving home on the day that Johnny painted on the floor, stopping at the traffic lights, starting again, with the road full of other cars in the late summer afternoon, cogitated. He wanted his wife to go with him to Vancouver Island and show the Island in all its summer beauty, for a whole week, to Hartley Pearce (the member for South Indigo and a coming Cabinet Minister) and Hartley's wife and his brother-in-law. It was not the kind of trip on which they could take Johnny, and he could not stay at home with the maid, who was a nitwit. Of course it would have been possible for Nora to leave Johnny with her sister (if she could) but Morgan Peake thought he had heard something about his sister-in-law going up-country to stay with some friends, and there was a man mixed up in it. Mr. Peake really liked Hartley Pearce and very much wished to take these people to the Island, ending up at Victoria, and it would be rather absurd if his wife who was considered to be a charming woman was unable to go with a future Cabinet Minister and his wife and brother-in-law because of her seven-year-old son who was in perfect health. Morgan Peake could not cogitate his way out of it, and, driving and stopping, driving and stopping, he arrived home, and hoped that they could come to some sensible arrangement.

While Morgan was driving home, Ellen Cuppy received a long telegram that breathed frustration and almost rage from beginning to end. The General Manager of George Gordon's firm was taken ill, and the Assistant Manager who had expected to fly west to meet Miss Cuppy, arriving next evening, had to stay in Montreal.

"How *revolting*!" said Ellen as she read the telegram about the General Manager. "How *revolting*!" The telegram revealed to her that she had counted serenely on the fulfilment of the plan to drive to the Okanagan together, and that at Naramata George would have met her great friends, Isa and Charles Cheney, and Isa Cheney and her husband would have met George Gordon. He will know me still better, she had thought, when he knows Isa and Charles, and I shall know him better in their company and know what he is like, I mean. In the company of these two people Ellen was always very happy. This was friendship, not of propinquity or convention, but of communication and love. Between Isa and Charles Cheney, and Gypsy Cuppy, and one or two more people whom she knew there was nothing which prevented communication or the unsaid word – nothing between. Their friendship was as clear as glass, as water, and as natural and refreshing as water. This particular friendship, which was old, was part of Ellen's life, ever since she had been Gypsy Cuppy, and she realized, as she looked down at the telegram, that her latent desire had been strong that she and George should be together with Charles and Isa, and that the clarity, and affection, and laughter of being with them would further reveal her (Ellen) to him, and would draw them still closer than all their chance meetings amongst acquaintances and good friends of the second order could possibly do. So, by taking away George and the drive to Naramata, and their arriving at the orchard, and by her intense and resentful disappointment, this telegram showed her that she truly loved him. Her mistrust of herself had gone, like the fog that it had been all the time: but the broken plan and the telegram had been needed to reveal this. She could think of nothing to answer. Revelation of herself in a telegram was impossible. She wired "How revolting", repeating herself, and that was what George read at his desk, and it compensated a little because it was like Ellen to say that.

The circle of life is extraordinary, and Miss Cuppy was drawn up into the circle of Mr. Prendergast's life when his secretary had to telephone the doctor that he was ill, and then telephone Mrs. Prendergast, and the doctor telephoned and made arrangements at the hospital, and the lives of George Gordon in Montreal and Miss Cuppy in Vancouver were affected, perhaps temporarily, or perhaps permanently and fatally. The dark girl, three thousand miles away, glowering at the paper in her hand, gave never a kind thought to the man whose serious operation was imminent and rendered his wife so desperate that when she telephoned the hospital again and they said his condition was "about" the same, the simple word "about" suddenly acquired appalling connotations to Mrs. Prendergast. If Ellen gave all this a thought, it was that it was very aggravating of Mr. Prendergast, and here were Ellen Cuppy and George Gordon prevented from driving to Naramata together. The fact that she had dilly-dallied with George for so long and now wanted to settle things immediately because a telegram had arrived did not strike Ellen as unreasonable. "Oh, what a pity," said Nora, when her sister showed her the telegram, pausing a moment in arranging the flowers to look toward Ellen.

What a *pity*! echoed Ellen furiously in thought, and said aloud, "Yes, isn't it unfortunate!" She was so cagey that she would not let her sister know how great was her disappointment; or perhaps the shock of the revelation of her love which the telegram had brought to her stunned her for the moment.

They went into the garden to get more flowers, and Ellen, going to the garden's edge, looked at False Creek. A small tug raced out in a hurry, bearing its bone in its mouth and leaving its white wake behind. Ellen stooped to pick the flowers. Although she was disappointed, she was excited by her revelation and everything looked more beautiful to her and the air of the garden was pleasant.

When Morgan Peake arrived and joined his family on the

grass he greeted them, "Norrah, my dear – ah, Gypsy!" and then he drew his wife aside and with as much policy as possible told her about the member for South Indigo and his wife and brother-in-law.

"What I really want to do, dolling," he said, "(they arrive on Tuesday) is to go at once to Nanaimo, drive them up-island as far as Comox at least – or perhaps into the Forbidden Plateau – and then back to Victoria. Hartley and I have quite a bit to do there, and you could run the others about for a day or two, couldn't you? You could drive out to Sooke and see the Hamiltons." He put his case simply, and left it on her doorstep, for he knew that her mind would fly to Johnny, who was of necessity a frequent veto, and she would do what she would do. She was aggravating, though handsome.

"Oh," she said, "that does sound nice, and of course I'd love to come" (she knew her duty, but how difficult a divided duty is, especially if the mind inclines one way) "but at the *moment* I don't really see . . . " and then she amazed her husband by saying brightly, "I don't know why I shouldn't try and see if Gypsy could possibly help us."

"But I thought she was going away."

"Yes, but she might come back a day or so early, and then she's going to Aunt Maury's. She might take Johnny with her."

What a remarkable woman she is, thought Morgan. Here I was, all ready to be turned down for no justifiable reason, and she surprises me.

"Don't say anything about her trip. Her young man has wired that he can't come. I don't know how she feels, she didn't say."

"Too bad, too bad," said Morgan, who did not mind one way or the other.

Nora wandered over to the garden edge and said, coughing a little, "Morgan's come home with a problem. He has to take some people from Ottawa to the Island next Tuesday for a week, and he really wants me to go – and I think I should. But if I go, what shall I do about Johnny! Bessie's too stupid to leave him with."

Ellen thought quickly that of course she could make arrangements to look after Johnny.

But first she said, "Send him to that little boys' camp – The Foxes they call it – at Comox."

"Oh no, I couldn't do that," said Nora. "Johnny has never been in a boys' camp, he would be homesick and I wouldn't be at home in case he wanted to leave The Foxes."

"Nora dear," said her sister gently, "let him be homesick."

Mrs. Peake gave her a look that relegated her. "I was wondering . . . " she said, and "Can I take him?" said Ellen at the same moment. "I can cut short my stay with Isa, and come down, and pick up Johnny and take him with me to Aunt Maury's. Anyone is safe with Aunt Maury there, and I promise you I'll be very careful of him. Uncle Dick might be there too."

She looked at her sister with her candid brown eyes wide open, and the lashes fringed back.

"I would feel so happy, so relieved, with you!" Nora murmured. "Oh, thank you, thank you, Gypsy. You *are* good! I'll go and tell Morgan. It is certainly the best solution."

Ellen Cuppy was a strong swimmer and careful. She was good in a boat. It was reasonable that Nora should trust her, especially with Aunt Maury there who had brought up three sons. Ellen was pleased, and her irritation had almost vanished. She still felt that the foxes were better than she could ever be. She nearly said to Johnny in the approved third-person formula "Will Johnny come with Aunty for a holiday?" and then she said to herself Idiot, speak English to the boy.

She said to him, "Do you want to come for a holiday with me?"

Johnny said "Oh Aunty!" and over his face ran the little preludes and pulses and ripples of thought and feeling gathering for expression . . . the soft flush came and receded . . . the eyes opened, then crinkled. Hang it all, little John, she thought, you'd better have been tough. It's easier than all this ecstasy.

"Is that where you said there were seals?"

"Yes, there are often seals. They hunt for salmon and

sometimes when they stop hunting under the water they come to the top and their heads rise out of the water with hardly a ripple and they look about them like nice dogs with round heads and big soft brown eyes and you'd really think they could talk and read. They are very inquisitive and when you're rowing they'll follow you along, and go down, and come up again nearer the boat or farther away. They look at you, and all of a sudden they're gone . . . "

"Will they look at me?"

"Yes. I think I can promise you that a seal will pop up his head and look at you."

"Oh, what will he think I am?"

"He might think you're a funny-looking Indian the wrong colour, because he often sees Indians sitting in boats, and you'll be sitting in a boat, but you'll be a pink colour and the Indians are brown. The Indians go along the shore slowly in a canoe or a rowboat or they go further out in little fishboats with an engine. They sleep on the fishboat. I sometimes think it would be nice to be an Indian, Johnny, don't you?" And that started her asking herself, Do I really? If you are an Indian do you begin thinking from a totally different premise? Do you then see the world and people differently and differently conditioned? How can we understand? and how can we legislate?

Thirty-Two

MR. PEAKE was in the habit of going to a certain place in White Rock, which is about an hour's run from Vancouver. When the House was sitting, and he was in Ottawa, he received a report each week from a Mr. and Mrs. Waldman, who lived in a small house not far from the sea, which had an enclosed garden and a little back yard.

With the visit to Victoria in view, and therefore with an immediate change of plans, he decided to leave his office early, which was not an easy matter, and drive to White Rock. On his way he stopped at a little general store with which he was familiar, and bought a red ball attached to a string, and a bag of bright innocuous candies. Again, as he approached White Rock, he stopped and bought a pint of ice-cream. They do not expect me, he said to himself, and the rather unfair thought came that they would have no opportunity to make special preparations for his coming and therefore he would see for himself whether his son Gilbert was still well cared for, and whether Thursday (Mr. Peake's usual day) was or was not the occasion for window-dressing. He had thought, drumming his fingers on his desk, perhaps I should telephone that I am coming. Then – not for the purpose of taking the Waldmans at a disadvantage but because a father may visit a son when it suits him – he left at once and arrived at the small house with the enclosed garden in the late afternoon. He lifted the latch of the gate with a feeling of uncertainty, and there was Gilbert sitting in his chair, looking much as usual, and

Mrs. Waldman working in her garden. The dog rushed up. The child looked at his father without recognition. Mrs. Waldman straightened herself and welcomed Mr. Peake. Everything, it seemed, was well – or as well as it could ever be.

Mrs. Waldman, who was a practical woman, a trained nurse, honest, well paid, and with a good heart, never became used to the visit of the heavily-built man, rather ponderous, who sat opposite the idiot boy, offering him a toy which the child sometimes took possession of, giving him a sweet which the child ate with relish, and then feeding him from the dish of ice-cream with more dexterity than she expected.

In the evening, when Gilbert was in bed, and Mr. Peake had long since arrived home, Mrs. Waldman would say something like this, from time to time, to her husband and daughter:

"I can't get over it and I never shall, how that man comes out to see his child and his wife never does. He's a wonderful person, that Mr. Peake." She felt resentful toward the mother, Mrs. Peake.

And her husband, if he said anything at all as he read the newspaper, said something like this: "You best not form opinions about what you know nothing about. The sight of Bertie to a sensitive woman and him never getting any better might be more than she could take. Maybe a man can take it more easy. They got another boy to look after, haven't they? You mind your own business and let them mind theirs."

"I still don't see how any woman can . . . " said Mrs. Waldman.

"The more do I," said their daughter, who did not care for the boarder.

Since Johnny's birth Nora had not ceased to put away from her the thought of the little mongol who was well cared for, washed, dressed, and fed by Mr. and Mrs. Waldman. It was as though she could not bear the darkness to fall upon Johnny. Her absence had continued very simply, naturally. As the time drew near for the birth of the child who was Johnny, Morgan had said, "I think you shouldn't go, dolling. I talked to Sykes, and he says unless you are very anxious to go, you shouldn't go", and Nora stayed at home, and Morgan drove alone to White Rock.

"Is he all right?" she would say, half fearfully.

"He's very well, nothing to worry about," Morgan would answer, and Nora told herself it was better for the baby that she should not go.

Then, when Johnny was born – she must not go. For months she must not go; soon it was established that it was not right for her to go; and although that was no longer true, the feeling remained that some day she would resume going, but not now. Later. Her heart was set on Johnny, her only son.

At last Morgan said to his wife, after much thought, "Norrah, my dear, Johnny must know Gilbert, you know." And Nora had answered, "Oh, Morgan . . . but it will be better later." And Morgan had said gravely, "It will be harder later. It may be too late. Shall I take him next time?" And Nora had said, "Not now . . . not this time . . . I can't expose Johnny yet to . . ."

Morgan was moved always by something that was pity and compunction and responsibility and paternity and therefore he visited his idiot son and drove there alone; he sat for a few minutes silent with the boy; he fed him; he drove home; and at last he took these visits as a matter of course, and did not speak of them to Nora. She was able to avert her mind and she did not speak; and because Johnny must be saved, and spared, and cherished, a blind was drawn down quite easily between her life at home with the cherub, and the child at White Rock. It is not my fault! she used to think in the early days with all the resentment of which she was capable. But now she had very nearly forgotten a situation which for some years had been accepted.

The fact that during all these years Morgan had gone to White Rock alone did not alienate him from his wife. Because he loved her, he spared her, and thought he had reason enough; he excused her also on account of her youth, not noticing that she was no longer young.

Into Morgan's life, brushing the edges from time to time,

came loping Nora's young sister Gypsy whom he accepted, not as a person, but as an appanage of Nora's. She was very good-looking, he believed, but he was not at home with young people in general. When Gypsy broke her engagement with his young half-brother Huw and fled to Saskatoon, although Morgan had for some time felt the natural inclination to side with Huw, he later had to admit to himself that the unpredictable Huw had nothing much but looks to commend him, and the girl had more sense than he gave her credit for. Gypsy had been aware of something existing in connection with Nora's poor little boy, but, as no one referred to him, she rather forgot him. She had been away so long at the war and at Saskatoon. She thought, once, that he must have died years ago, and that no one liked to say so, and she had not thought again. If she had known of Morgan's visits she would have been deeply touched, and would have looked at him with informed and interested eyes. Because she had forgotten the existence of the child at White Rock she was critical of her sister's absorption in the cherub, and on the cherub's behalf. So, as things were, Ellen was sometimes crotchety and Nora dwelt apart, with the blind drawn down; and this was owing to the little cipher sitting in seclusion in Mrs. Waldman's back garden at White Rock, ministered to by Morgan.

Thirty-Three

ON THE EVENING of the day that Ellen received George's telegram, Nora came into Ellen's bedroom in a blue dressing-gown, with a hairbrush in her hand. She said nothing but began brushing her hair this way, that way, with strong strokes. Her face was in shadow but her hair stood like a frightened nimbus round her head. She has come to talk about arrangements, thought Ellen, who said, "I'll get the boat schedule. They go three times a week. I'll be back from Naramata in time. I think they go on a Tuesday", but Nora paid no attention. She stopped brushing her hair and said, looking down at the hairbrush, "I'd better tell you something."

Ellen sat on the side of her bed.

"I wouldn't tell you this," said Nora slowly, still looking down, "only if you're taking Johnny you should know." Ellen waited.

Nora looked up. "D'you remember the winter before last, I wrote and told you Johnny had a cold?"

Well, what on earth, said Ellen to herself. She was one of those people who do not regard a cold as news. If a cold occurs in a letter, skip it and let's get on with the news. So she said nothing. In any case, she did not remember that Johnny had had a cold two winters ago. She thought her elder sister was getting stupider and stupider.

"You would notice," said Nora, speaking with hesitation,

"that I didn't mention it again . . . I'll tell you now." Ellen waited.

"He had this cold," said Nora, coughing a little, "and then he had infections. In his ears. In the middle ear. The infection cleared up. And then I began to notice that Johnny didn't seem to hear very well. Perhaps you've noticed. I took him to the doctor again. He didn't say much . . . I was very much annoyed. He practically only told me to bring him back at a certain time. Well, I did. He told me Johnny would lose his hearing. He'd be deaf."

"How awful!" said Ellen. "How could he! He might never be deaf at all! How can they tell!"

Nora continued sombrely. "I insisted on another opinion. I made them both tell me. I insisted. They tried to let me down easily . . . they said that perhaps, with some study . . . I wouldn't listen to that kind of thing. I had to know the very worst . . . I insisted on frankness. I *have* to know everything about him, Gypsy," she said in a broken voice, "*everything* about Johnny – all his present and his future, everything that any doctor, any person, might ever know about him. I have to know it all . . . "

Ellen, looking at her changed sister, wanted to say, "You mustn't, you can't", but she could not say it.

"Oh, Nolly" was all she could say. And then she thought as she saw how deeply her sister was suffering – all this high tragedy, isn't it out of proportion? A little boy is rather deaf, listening so charmingly, not quite hearing. A little boy is going to be a deaf man. It is too bad; but there are worse things.

"Nora," she said, returning to now and next week, "I will take good care of him. Especially now that I know he doesn't always hear. I will be so careful."

"Don't say that," said Nora sharply, "I can't even bear those words . . . 'that he doesn't always hear' . . . " and Gypsy saw in a flash of illumination that it was unendurable to her sister, sitting there in her blue dressing-gown, that her son, her little god, at that moment sleeping, should be touched, at all, ever, by a deprivation, a human limitation of any kind, and that anyone, ever, could perhaps pity him.

"Oh, Nolly," she said – and in these moments the old name, not spoken since childhood, came to her unnoticed, "I am ... oh, I can't tell you how sorry. I didn't know ... and it may never be, and if it is ... why, Nolly, he's a lovely child, he has everything else in the world, and there are worse things!"

"Don't talk like that," said Nora harshly. "It's plain you never had a child. It's easy to bear other people's troubles. I've heard that before and it's true." They had come a long way from the kind aunt taking the little nephew for a holiday.

"You won't speak of this," commanded Nora, "not to anyone, not to Morgan or anyone. Of course Morgan does not know ... "

"What!" Ellen exclaimed, and began to say You did not tell him! But she stopped. Everything was disproportionate and unnatural.

Nora composed herself.

"You see," she said, looking earnestly at her sister, "the minute you admit something, it exists and can become worse. I thought it all out – Morgan was away at the time. I thought, now, if I say nothing, it will not exist. Not even Johnny will realize, yet. But if it is admitted by Morgan, by Bessie, and then by other people that Johnny is becoming deaf – that would be intolerable – and it would become true, or true too soon. And it might never be true after all! So except in a corner of my mind, I refused to admit it. I said quite often and quite sharply to Bessie, 'Do you know, Bessie, you are beginning to speak indistinctly. You must speak more clearly,' and she does. But Morgan ... " and for a minute she seemed to be pondering. Then she said, "You see, he is so good ... he does everything for Gilbert. I must say he's ... " She rose, sighing.

What is she talking about?

"'Gilbert?'" said Ellen stupidly. "But who's Gilbert?"

"*Ellen!*" Nora exclaimed, staring shocked at her sister; and in that instant Ellen knew who Gilbert was. Of course he lived and had a name. Her blindness, her stupidity, and her own imperception silenced her.

Nora stood, with her hand on her cheek. Then whe went to the door. "You'll be good to him," she murmured.

"Oh, Nolly!" said Ellen, running to her. They clung together for a moment and what had seemed a little ridiculous but a short time ago was clear and tragical.

Ellen lit a cigarette and went out of a door that opened from her bedroom on to a balcony. To the east all the bright neon signs which were massed around the head of the bridge across the creek shone garish and changing and beautiful in reflection in the black creek. Lights showed a small moving tug pulling a darker object on the dark water. What had been tragedy became, on consideration, sad, proportionate, and complicated. Surely Nora was the answer because of her griefs and because her understanding had not usually extended to other people; now she had to suffer, and she and Morgan were – it seemed – alone and perhaps apart. Ellen felt very tenderly toward the little boy. It is a good thing I know, she said to herself, though I know now that I don't know Morgan, nor about Gilbert; you are walking along through the grasses on the cliff top, admiring the pretty view, when – crack crack.

In all the houses whose lights I see across the creek are there unexpected reticences and blow-ups happening? Not in all of them and not all the time; to none of us all the time. What a relief it will be, she felt, turning away from the reticences in this house, to see George who has so much common sense. We will have nothing of that kind between us. What one of us knows, the other will know.

Oh yes, of course we shall have to have reticences. My poor Nora; and she went back into the house.

Thirty-Four

ELLEN BEGAN her drive alone from Vancouver to Naramata early on a day that promised to be hot. She preceded morning traffic up the Fraser Valley to Chilliwack and arrived at Hope long before mid-morning. She took the road to the right and made good speed while travel on the road was still light.

Climbing, she passed innocent mountain streams with numerical names, such as Nine Mile Creek, Seventeen Mile Creek, Twenty-three Mile Creek. Optimists make their way up those tangled streams and, contented as cats or seraphs, cast the fly. Ellen drove on between the forested banks and over Sunday Summit, skirting the Similkameen River which flows in these parts with a changing story, and into the Keremeos Valley which was too hot. It was all very well for a fruit country no doubt, but for Ellen the heat was uncomfortable, striking from the hot air, up from the road, down from the hills, and ripening the apples and peaches as desired. No one in Keremeos village appeared to notice the heat, and perhaps the chief reason why Ellen disliked it was that she was prevented from concentrating completely on George, with whom, she decided, she had always been in love. She drove well, too fast, automatically, and thought chiefly of George.

Ever since the first night that he had telephoned to her, speaking as a stranger introduced by a friend, ever since they had been together in Saskatoon, had had dinners together, and he had given her those books, this had been ordained.

Ever since I first ran to the telephone or opened the door, I have loved him, she thought lyrically, driving along the valley. This was not true; but the radiance of the fact that she loved George and was not afraid any more to marry him, spread around and forward and backward, illuminating areas of her life which had nothing whatever to do with the matter; and this is one of the perquisites of love.

Early in the afternoon she reached the road that overlooks Skaha Lake and drove down through Penticton and toward Naramata between the peach trees above the Okanagan Lake. She made a turn to the left and into the orchard that belonged to Isa's husband Charles.

The peach-growing sun blazed down upon the opposite blue hills and the too-dazzling water of the lake and the peach orchards, and on Isa and Ellen moving into the shade under the trees and saying it was much too hot but how lovely to be here. Birds must have swooned or slept, for there was no birdsong in the air. Droves of children – Isa's children and others – ran regardless between the trees, wearing nothing much, came running and asking and disappearing down toward the lake. Splashings and cries of children came all the time from the lake edge. Charles was somewhere in the orchards, doing very well although he had only one hand. His hand was blown off in the war, but neither he nor Isa nor the children seemed to look upon this as anything out of the way, or a disability.

I shall tell Isa all about George, Ellen had thought as she drove between the hills; she is the one person I can tell.

Her eyes strayed around the peach trees with their green velvet fruit beginning to be stained richly, as she thought with pleasure of telling Isa about George. But suddenly, seeing the red roof of a house among distant trees, "Oh, is Merri Thompson here?" she said, remembering last time, and fearing.

Isa laughed. "No. God is good. Merri is across the lake at Summerland with her mother-in-law."

Peace descended again, whole peace unflecked by the fear of Merri Thompson arriving between the trees " . . . oh my dear . . . why hello, here's Ellen! when d'you get here? . . .

has Annabel decided to stick it? Poor Fred, *he's* the one *I'm* sorry for . . . I've *tons* of questions to ask you . . . Isa, you know Tuesday? my dear it was a scream . . . marrafact I nearly died when he told me, because of course I knew what Guy had said and of course *I* knew and the others didn't that it wasn't rye at all and there was Dorthy . . . " on and on and Isa thinking Is my face becoming glazed or what. She is good, she is kind, she is pretty, but *will* she stop talking for the space of one breath so that we can see the summer afternoon again . . . no, she will not; she can destroy the summer afternoon and Ellen and me as well quite easily.

" . . . so Chas said oh you make me tired, he was fit to be tied, but marrafact he's crazy about Dorthy so they put it in the oven . . . " (in the oven?). People are defenceless before her. The air becomes constipated with words. She should have her meter read. Where is the summer afternoon? It has withdrawn itself. That is what Merri Thompson can do to a summer day.

But now Merri was not coming to disturb, because she has a mother-in-law whom Allah preserve, and after silences and remarks and the happy being-together, Ellen began to tell Isa about George Gordon, because the late sun was declining, and some at least of the children picnicking on the beach might soon come calling through the trees.

"Of course George would have come," said Ellen, "but at the last minute some hateful man called Prendergast, George's boss I think, was ill, and so George had to stay. He could have been ill any other time and it wouldn't have mattered," she said inconsiderately, ignoring Mr. Prendergast's danger and his wife's distress and everything that concerned his care and comfort. "Isn't it enraging," stretching herself in the sun-dappled shade. "No, it almost isn't enraging, Isa, it's so lovely to be here at last. But I may as well tell you, I've decided to marry George."

Isa and Ellen sat under the trees of the orchard and Isa leaned forward and Ellen talked. " . . . and then when he sent me those books and now when he is so truly concerned about Mr. Platt and me and with what is happening I knew he was different again. But this time, Isa, I'm not afraid – I really couldn't bear it if anything happened to stop me marrying George . . . that proves it. I couldn't bear it."

"But," said Isa, sitting up very straight, "what's he like?"

"I'm telling you what he's like," said Ellen. "I told you that when I first met him in Saskatoon . . ."

"No, I want to know what he's *like*!"

"Well," said Ellen slowly, contemplating the light and shade, "if it comes to eyes and noses it's hard to say. He's taller than I am and I think he may have been a gangling boy but he doesn't gangle now . . . but how hard it is to tell about eyes and noses . . . There's no doubt, my dear, that the human face . . ."

"Is his nose long or short or red?"

"Red! Oh my goodness no . . . once I tried to tell someone what Mother was like and I couldn't. You can describe strangers quite fearlessly, but when it comes to someone special . . . I could only say about Mother that she was little, and full of light, and then when it came to hair – brownish, and eyes – brownish, and lively and intelligent – and still that didn't tell anything about her . . . and it's like that with George . . . his eyes are lively and intelligent and good to talk to . . ."

"Eyes are?" murmured Isa indulgently. "There's a poem 'thine in mine eyes' . . . something . . . so I'll not know what he's like till I see him, Gypsy?"

"No," said Ellen, smiling. "But believe me, Isa, I'm content and I think I've never known what it is to be content before."

Isa stood up. She saw her husband coming through the trees, tanned leather-brown to the waist. "Come in while I get supper," she said, very happy.

Ellen stayed at Naramata with Charles and Isa for three days instead of five days. She wrote to George her unqualified yes. Then she drove back to Vancouver because of Johnny and because of Mr. Hartley Pearce who might be a Cabinet Minister some day. The change of plan now caused her no concern; anything that would happen between now and George's arrival was immaterial because her mind was set.

Thirty-Five

MRS. DICK PEAKE, who was Morgan's Aunt Maury although she was younger than Morgan, had a summer cottage on the top of one of the many rocky points of Galiano Island. It was rather sheltered by cedar trees. It looked down one way on to Active Pass which separates Galiano Island from Mayne Island, and on the other side it looked down on a small sheltered crevice between points of land which is almost a little bay. This little bay or cove makes possible some swimming, and a good deal of sunbathing. It is good to lie on the dry moss on the upper part of the cove with the sun beating down beneficently. Even the sunlight is scented with cedar and juniper. The juniper bush lies flattened and neatly sprawled against the ground. It has great elegance. Its colour is subdued, a green which is also grey and there may be purple in its shadows. Its scent is aromatic and recalls the scent of the sage-brush in the Upper Country. Its texture is strong and defensive but it can be approached. Year after year Mr. and Mrs. Dick Peake and their sons and Isa and Gypsy and other people had sat on the ground beside this juniper bush, idly breaking off a fragment and crushing it in their fingers, looking out to sea, jumping up, running down for a swim, coming up to cast themselves down in the sun to dry near the juniper bush. So the juniper bush was part of their summers. It lived on and on, strong and elegant, through storm and sun.

They could not swim far because they had to stay pretty well within the little cove on account of the tides that flow in powerful and uncertain streaks toward and from Active Pass. They never swam on the Active Pass side. It would be dangerous. So they swam within the confines of the little bay, but they rowed beyond the bay.

Sprung in strange attitudes from these rocky and piney shores are arbutus trees. People on the Pacific Coast know the arbutus tree well. It is called in California the madrona because of the Spanish history. In British Columbia it is called arbutus, which is its family name. The arbutus tree grows, each year, a skin like bark; or, one should say more correctly, its smooth surface, of a green which ranges in a shade near chartreuse, becomes deeper in shade and hardens into a skin, a bark of glorious copper colour. When the morning sun strikes the smooth trunk of an arbutus tree the copper glows, and anyone looking up suddenly at the arbutus tree exclaims aloud; and remembers. This copper bark, as the year advances, splits, peels, curls, and floats away, revealing below it the young green again. Since the leaves of the tree become dry and fall fairly continuously for a time, the arbutus tree is not suitable for the ordinary garden unless the owner of the garden likes cleaning up after his pets every day for a season of the year that seems endless; and since the arbutus tree is difficult to transplant, one seldom sees it in the ordinary garden which is a good thing, as it there resembles the noble savage in a drawing-room. In such places as Victoria (only there are no such places) gardeners accept this pleasant toil, for the arbutus flourishes on the shores of Victoria which so often constitute the rocky gardens of that charmer among small cities.

There is one more thing that should be said about the arbutus tree. It is, sometimes, more human than anything in the vegetable world and is certainly nobler than the mandrake. There is one arbutus tree on Aunt Maury Peake's point whose trunk is as large as a human body (the trunk is usually more slender); it divides as at a groin, a shoulder. The smooth curves, held firmly by the two hands, are like living sculpture of the human body – copper thigh, abdomen, flank, muscle; you expect a lift as of the tree's green breathing.

Since the cove at Uncle Dick and Aunt Maury's cottage faces west they see the beginning, the whole, and the last of the sunset. Every summer, as night comes on, the collection of visitors – one, two, ten – sprawl or sit on the dry moss, and, looking through the arbutus tree, watch the sky go wild. Aunt Maury thought and spoke on one such night in that very summer that Ellen took Johnny there, of the "Amen" at the end of Rossini's Stabat Mater. There was the first melodious affirmation, darkening clouds in the sky; then there was the glory from horizon to zenith; then came the solemn affirmation, the final statement "Amen, Amen, this day is done", and there was night.

On the Active Pass side of the cottage is a small steep ravine that separates it, except by sea or by climbing down to the beach and up again, from a shack, which was owned and lived in by Mr. Abednego. Mr. Abednego was a nice man, dirty, old, with a ragged beard. He had a rowboat with an inboard engine, and a fishboat. He was what was called a permanent resident, that is, he lived there. Mrs. Peake was gregarious in town but not in the country, so the small ravine suited her very well. She and Mr. Abednego were on the best possible terms, but Mr. Abednego watched Mr. and Mrs. Peake and their friends at a distance at all hours with a consuming curiosity which they satisfied, up to a point, but it could become tiresome, discussing the distant neighbours or their own families at all times of day. Mr. Abednego would depart and soon return remarking, "Say, Miss Cuppy, I never ast you about your brother-in-law Peake. He's a smart fella that. Is he a Senator or ain't he? Would he be fifty-five perhaps? Sixty perhaps?" and she would say, "Yes, he would." "Wife's quite a bit younger, they tell me," Mr. Abednego would say. "Oh yes, quite a bit younger." "A nice woman they say." "Very, *very* nice", and Mr. Abednego would go away and think that one over for a while. This passionate interest in the summer visitors was understandable in Mr. Abednego as three parts of his year were lonely. "I'll keep him off when you come up, Dick," said Aunt Maury.

"No," said Mr. Peake, "I like Abednego,"

Across from this rather isolated rocky bench by the sea, with the two cottages, was Mayne Island where there was a good wharf. Rather large boats called there. The shores of these many many islands in the Gulf of Georgia are variations of Mrs. Peake's little cove, one way or another, little or big. On a flight from Vancouver to Victoria the traveller looks down on those innumerable tree-filled islands of dark green colour, and sees occasional clearings with soft green pastures or orchards, a white farm or outbuildings. The traveller thinks, Down below me is a life which is idyllic, and so, from the air, it would seem. But life on ever so beautiful an island can cease to be an idyll when the island is storm-bound, or repairs cannot be made, or the baby is born, or the boat's engine breaks down incurably and one cannot afford a new one, or the dweller becomes bored. Nevertheless, life on these islands must be as nearly idyllic as life can be. There lie these jewelled islands on the ocean. The crooked shores are laced with a thin line of foam, of spume, as white as marble. Then comes a setting of translucent jade green where the ocean is shallow, and then the ocean on which you look down resumes its depth and solid blue, streaked with tides, flecked with wrinkled waves. There go the toy tugs, apparently immobile for all their going, and behind them are toy booms and rafts of logs which the airborne traveller will have to believe are gigantic. Away stream the vees which are the lines made in the water by the passage of the boats, great and small. Look intently at the jewelled islands; so short is the flight over the islands of the Gulf of Georgia to Victoria, and then they are gone.

This, then, was the place to which Gypsy and Johnny went; it was old to her and new to him. She would rather Johnny had been one among the other foxes near Comox, where there was a safe wide beach, and a sand spit, and young men, casual yet watchful, who were there to see that the foxes ran about and swam about and rowed about, and came to no harm. But he was not with the other foxes, he was with Mrs. Peake and Gypsy Cuppy, and however nice they were, they were not as good as the foxes.

Thirty-Six

ELLEN AND Johnny went that fine morning on the big boat that calls at the Government Wharf at Mayne Island, and there they left the big boat and saw it disappear round the point, and by and by the old fishboat belonging to Mr. Abednego came chugging across from Galiano Island. Nora had restrained herself well when she left home, especially as she was performing the adult job of entertaining three strangers and it would have been a little absurd to be anything but nonchalant at leaving Johnny with Gypsy for a week. Nevertheless Ellen knew that the major part of her was repeating, Johnny is leaving me for the first time, and only the mechanical part of her mind was occupied for the moment with the business of entertaining and pleasing Morgan's friends who would be entertained and pleased.

Johnny was unmoved at leaving home, but very much moved and excited at going away to Aunt Maury's. He could not have told anyone what he expected to see and why he was particularly set on seeing a seal or seals. Probably he had some picture book of seals; he felt, Ellen was sure, that seals were as nearly wild and romantic animals as he might ever see, and they were safely removed by the element of water; and he was a little boy to whom even cats and dogs were almost wild animals, or, at least, unknown. As they sat on the wharf waiting for Mr. Abednego's boat coming nearer and nearer he said and said again, "Aunty, is this where there are seals?

"Not here so much," said Ellen, "but out there in the deep

water, further out near the other island, near Aunt Maury's cabin . . . see, near that green point!"

"Near Aunt Maury's cabin," repeated Johnny, sitting beside her on some piled wood, very good and biddable. What a pretty little boy he is, holding his canvas zipper bag, sometimes jigging up and down for joy. See, there is another little boy. He is lying on his stomach at the wharf edge looking down into the water along a fishing line. He may catch a shiner. Other children come running and skipping down the wharf and a young man strides purposefully. He is serious. The gulls and the children laugh and scream. White gulls laugh sarcastically and wheel and scream above every little wharf on this coast of British Columbia, above every wharf in the world, and every ocean. How do they fill their stomachs, thinks Ellen, these gulls, these scavengers, and keep up their strength for flying, eternally flying? The sun shines and the trees glow green and the sea sparkles in Active Pass between the two islands; nobody works, one would think (one cannot see into the kitchen of the white wooden hotel), certainly not the young man who is tinkering with his boat; he is doing what he enjoys most of all. The island tempo, the dreaming-on-a-wharf tempo, pervades and prevails. Not too near the edge, Johnny! Sit lazily on the wharf unimpatient in the sunshine and the sea-sparkle and the gull-cries, waiting for Mr. Abednego whose face they see now among its whiskers.

Mr. Abednego's fishboat smelled so strongly of fish and gas and oil and tar and Mr. Abednego that even the sweet air of Active Pass could not blow the smell away; yet everyone liked it when Mr. Abednego shouted and waved to Come on in, although he was often profane. Today, as they approached the western shore of Galiano Island and the little crooked indentation that served as a haven and protected the fishboat from both east and west, they saw Aunt Maury Peake standing on the small headland above the anchorage waving, and the wind blew her hair and blew her skirt back against her, outlining her circumference.

"So you're a member of parlyment's boy, hay?" said Mr. Abednego. "You'll have to grow some. Better get your aunty let you come along fishing with me. You like to go fishing, hay? Got any old close? Can't wear them good close."

"Yes, Mr. Abd . . . " said Johnny politely, looking very clean. "I'll come if Aunty says," he said, looking at Ellen.

But she was waving to Aunt Maury and getting ready to lift out the gunny sacks with the extra flannelette sheets and the stores. Mr. Abednego beached the boat a bit against some huge driftwood and she climbed out, helping Johnny ahead of her, and then turned to lift out the things. Johnny ran up the short slope and then Ellen remembered that she had brought Mr. Abednego a roast and a cake, and she undid the mouth of a gunny sack and took them from the top where they lay.

"Well, whaddaya know," said Mr. Abednego very nicely by way of thanks. The Peakes paid him money at the end of the season, but the family – or those who counted as family – always brought him something tasty. The whole arrangement was excellent, and Mr. Abednego was thereby kept in touch with all of them personally, not entirely out of devotion, but because he liked unbearably to know what they were up to. Every move of theirs was visible to him and entertaining; but still the gully was convenient, lying between.

When Johnny ran up the slope, Aunt Maury bent and kissed him. Ellen followed, making a double journey of hauling the bags and the gunny sacks.

"See you later, Miss Cuppy," said Mr. Abednego, sheering the fishboat away from the driftwood out into deep water again, and she knew she would.

There was a little room where Johnny would sleep. Aunt Maury and Ellen would sleep on the verandah overlooking the Pass, and in the night they would lie awake too long watching the lights moving up and down the Pass. Is that a tug? Yes, it moves slowly, and see the light at the end of the boom of logs, and the lights that twinkle brightly against the dark mass of Mayne Island, which are lights in people's houses – and the stars; and then they drift asleep.

When in the morning small chores were done, Aunt Maury and Ellen sat or lay and continued to lie on the mossy pine-needled ground looking out to sea and Johnny climbed down to the little bay facing west, where they could keep an eye on him while they talked.

As always on a hot day the scent arose from the juniper and the cedars (the arbutus trees seem to have no scent or perhaps human beings do not smell it) and from the deposit of pine needles which yearly are assimilated by the ground, and from the seaweed and salt sea (less strong), and these scents evoked summers gone away and summers to come. Ellen had noticed scents of a land before. When she and Father went on the voyage through the Panama Canal to Antwerp, as they neared Panama City a sullen air blew from the city and carried a stench as of decay. The air was hot, humid, heavy in itself, and heavy with this smell. When she was in the city she observed no stench at all, and next day as they proceeded down the Canal between jungly banks there came a sweet richness in the air from the lush warm meaningless vegetation. There must have been death there too, because many huge carrion birds floated high and low. She knew then that she was a northerner, and only a visitor to such strange smells and places.

The time was coming, that morning at Galiano, when she must go down and swim and gentle Johnny along in the water of the little bay, and she would do that each morning and afternoon until by the end of their week which was to last over the weekend Johnny would go home a swimmer, perhaps, with confidence to slide off the rock into the water, go under and emerge, shaking his head, and he would dog-paddle across the tiny bay without fear, and Ellen would be proud. She looked down idly at Johnny who ran into the water and then ran out, squealing – not for fear, but for the love of squealing that water generates in children. But for the moment she pushed away any intimation of something to be done, and lay there on the moss in eternal summer afternoon, thinking chiefly about George and about some summer days when they would be here together.

Aunt Maury and she would join Johnny yelling and paddling and splashing, and then she and Aunt Maury would dive – even Aunt Maury would dive – off the rocks and swim to the mouth of the bay but not beyond; and they would sit in the sunshine on a half-submerged rock where the limpets expanded and contracted in the water washing up and down.

Johnny was not made special and he took his demotion easily. Ellen was much aware of him for Nora's sake and for his own sake, but she did not show it, and he took third place in the household. When they rowed outside the bay towards the Pass he learned to sit still in the boat. Ellen was watchful of his fair skin. He admired and loved Mr. Abednego in spite of his dirt, language and whiskers ("Hay, Miss Cuppy! Tell that young one to get a move on and I'll take you all up along up the shore . . . So your pa's in parlyment, hay? That's how he earns his living, hay? Now what time d'you suppose he'd get up in the morning now?"), and they all went out with him in his boat. Johnny, always timorous, was not afraid with Mr. Abednego. They were men together, and looks and language were part of the boat and the waves and the fine morning.

There was the rest of Tuesday, and then there was Wednesday, and Thursday and Friday came; but you do not count by days which slide, shimmer, coalesce, and become one summer day in such a place.

Johnny had not seen a seal.

Thirty-Seven

AUNT MAURY PEAKE was (indeed is) a remarkable person. She comes from Nova Scotia, of a line of sailing-ship builders, sea captains of the days of sail, Canadian mothers and grandmothers who bore their children at sea. Salt water, it seems, is really in her veins, and salt water is salt water whether it be in the Atlantic Ocean or the Pacific Ocean. Aunt Maury took some time to rank the Pacific Ocean equal to the Atlantic Ocean in her affections, but, once done, the British Columbia coast with its history was hers. She blesses everything she touches, with fun perhaps, or a loaf of homemade bread, or You stay here tonight and I'll give you a hot toddy and you'll be all right in the morning, or simply with Yes, I understand; or just with being somewhere in the house. She is intelligent. She is short and square. She wears improbable hats. She is good company. She can be silent. After all that is said, there remain her preferences. Her first preference after her family is Captain George Vancouver.

The first night that Ellen and Johnny were at her cottage, and Johnny was asleep in his room, Aunt Maury under the light of the lamp said, "See this book? I've got it at last. I've been hunting it for ages. It's out of print. It's just come. See? It's a *Walbran*" (what's a Walbran?), and under the lamplight in the dark cottage Aunt Maury, leaning over her book at the table, told Ellen about Captain George Vancouver sailing these indented and unknown shores from south to north, and charting and naming them (their names and charts remain to this day) "for us who have followed so easily after," she said. "Except for some Spanish and Indian names," she said, tapping the book with her fingers, "most of the names of channels and shoals and points and islands on our coast are names of English sailors of all ranks, or names of the English sailing ships, or names from their Home." And Aunt Maury said with scorn, "And I read some ignoramus scoffing at the Englishry of this west coast! These came and named the names, as French and Scottish and English did on the Atlantic coast, and who would dare to scoff at *them*! Two – four – years away from home in their toy ships, charting Antarctica and the shores and reefs of Australia and New Zealand and the Sandwich Islands as they came along, and these shores too, and by God," said this daughter of sea captains, "Captain Cook charted the dangerous foggy shores of Labrador, and more. It didn't matter whether they were seaman or Admiral – they knew the sea and the stars and the weather and the rocks and shoals and no one better, before or since, and not much in the way of instruments." She opened the shabby green covers.

"Listen to the good plain rational seaman's English," she said, "how got they their education, these men, shipping to sea as little boys? Here, listen to Captain Vancouver in his Journal of 1792, naming Mount Baker – you know Mount Baker, Ellen – 'As the day advanced, the wind, which as well as the weather was delightfully pleasant, accelerated our progress along the shore. About this time a very high conspicuous craggy mountain presented itself towering . . . '"

Aunt Maury looked up at Ellen, but as it was plain that Ellen was not listening to Captain Vancouver's Journal, she closed the book, murmuring, however, "Everyone calls that peak Mount Baker and no one cares why. Captain Vancouver was a very great seaman. He sailed back to his native land and died too soon and too young."

But what is she talking about, thought Ellen, looking intelligent and returning rapidly from George Gordon and Montreal and George's flat which she had never seen, which he had suggested they should live in at first if she would marry him.

"It's fascinating!" she said, as good guest. How I love Aunt Maury, she thought; she has a fine plain face like a ship's figurehead – blunt nose and chin and the lamplight shining on it, all weather-stained.

But however much she loved Aunt Maury, she did not tell her about George. She thought continually of the time when Mr. Prendergast would be well again and they could plan, and George could come, and then of course life would be happy and endless – opening like a fan (never shockingly closing in death). Yet she could not speak of George, although she had done so to Isa, but that was different; she was habitually impulsive; yet she remained very cagey.

Mrs. Peake, looking at Ellen with bright lamplit eyes, was fully aware that she had not been listening.

"And what are you smiling at?" asked Ellen.

Thirty-Eight

AS AN AUNT who had promised seals, Ellen was a failure. There had always been seals resembling nice round-headed dogs in the waters of Active Pass, and that indicated the presence of salmon which these brown-eyed innocents decimated, taking a bite out of the belly of the salmon and letting it go. But that year there was never a seal. It was a poor salmon year, Mr. Abednego said.

Ellen knew that with all the godlikeness of being a man with the profane Mr. Abednego, with all the new largesse of summer and sea, something was lacking to Johnny if a seal did not raise its round head from the waters of Active Pass, look brightly at him, and sink vertically, leaving not a ripple with water closing over, as promised. It was important to him for reasons of his own that his joy should be replete by saying, "And we saw seals!" So she was glad when he came rushing down toward the beach on Friday afternoon crying out that there was a seal he was sure it was a seal and let's go out in the boat.

Ellen was sitting in the little rowboat that they kept in the small swimming bay and was disentangling a fishing line that someone had thrown down in a heap, picking at it and picking at it in the sunshine and the boat wobbling pleasantly with the water. She looked up and saw that Johnny running down the beach had his top bare. In spite of all care he had a nasty sunburn on his shoulders, so she called out, "Put on your shirt, you must put on your shirt if we're going on the water... No, I said Put on Your Shirt!"

"Oh," wailed Johnny, turning obediently and running up the slope and wailing that they would miss the seals. By the time that Ellen had tucked the tangled line into the bow and pulled to shore, Johnny was down again, wriggling into his shirt and scrambling into the boat at the same time.

"Where was it, Johnny?" she asked, pulling away.

"It was two seals it was you know where Mr. Abednego's place is, well, further out and to the right no the left I knew it was seals though it looked like knobs of wood because one went down and didn't make a ripple like you said. Oh hurry, hurry, Aunty!"

Ellen pulled hard on the oars and rounded the point of their bay and into Active Pass, rowing in the direction where Johnny had seen the seals. She looked back from time to time and there were no seals but there might be at any minute.

"Can you see one now?" But she could tell from his face that he did not. They rowed along.

The expression of his face changed, but he said nothing and continued to scan the water.

She rowed more slowly now. She hardly needed to row because she realized that the tide was with her, flowing fairly fast, and if she went too far she might find it hard to row back.

A look of surprise came on Johnny's face and he opened his mouth. He raised himself, half standing. "Sit down!" his aunt said sharply.

She stopped rowing, and looked around. The *Princess Elizabeth*, bound for Victoria, had entered the Pass. This was what Johnny had seen, but, compared with the departed seals, the large ship to which he was accustomed had had no significance. And then he had seen something else.

A terrifying thing was happening. The *Princess* steamed on and passed them, and in the channel of Active Pass her wash raised a great wave which, as Ellen looked, clashed against the now racing tide and rose in a wall of water which fell and broke. The succeeding wave of the ship's wash was nearer them now; it also met the oncoming tide, clashed, rose in a wall and fell. She tried to turn the boat. She rowed desperately against the tide which was flowing increasingly strongly with her but she could make not an inch – it seemed – against it. The next impact of the tide and wash rose near them and the falling wall of water, breaking as it fell, spattered Johnny who, gripping the sides of the boat, was half turned.

"Oh," he cried, and began to babble. Ellen rowed furiously but the powerful tide carried her on. She could see what was about to happen and there was no escaping. The succeeding wave raced toward them, hit the tide at their bow, rose in a wall and fell upon them. She had a sight of Johnny's terrified face amid the spray. She knew that he sprang stumbling toward her crying, "Aunty, Aunty!" She knew that she cried out, "Stay still! Don't move!" but the boat was over now and Johnny was in the swirling water and the oars were out of the rowlocks and she was in the water and blinded and thinking only Johnny, Johnny! Where are you? What a fool I am! Oh Nora, what a fool! Where is he? Oh Nora!

The push of the tide and the strength of the commotion of the ship's wave made ordinary swimming impossible, and as she struck out this way and that under water with the water and against the water reaching out her hands for the boy she was aware even then of the deepest anguish mixed inextricably with the bursting feeling in her lungs and her fighting the power of the tide and wash under the surface and her hunting blindly in the water for Johnny. She was Nora and Nora was herself, fighting in the water to grab hold of Johnny touching and losing and touching again and slipping from her fingers, grab hold, this way that way, the shirt – the slipping arm the empty water the wrenched arm the shirt – aah! something had struck her on the face and her lungs would burst and up they went hold him don't let him go what have I done to you. Her head above below the water, the clashing wave was clashing somewhere else and now she struck out somewhere with one arm and with the other held Johnny – clutching pulling down. Is this drowning? Will it be drowning? I sea-boy. How long does it last? Nora, he's slipping! How long does this last?

When something else entered the world and clawed at Johnny and took him, and the girl's head came above water again, she, breathless, seemed to see that Mr. Abednego heaved and pulled and yanked Johnny or some limp thing over the side of the fishboat and into the boat. She reached out and caught a bumper, an old tyre, that had come loose and had fallen. Something hit her again. Something hot blinded her. She put up a hand and found that it was blood.

Mr. Abednego turned and chugged the fishboat into the anchorage. She held on. Her head hurt. She did not know where the rowboat was, or the oars. The *Princess* had disappeared round the end of the Pass. Less than an hour ago she had been rocking in the bay and this had not been dreamed of. She was consumed with the misery of her folly, for she knew that before going into Active Pass she should have made sure of the tides, and she knew, too, that the *Princess* went through the Pass at this time. But is there any time in this place?

Johnny lay quite still in Mr. Abednego's boat. Ellen did not know how long they had been in the water, a few minutes or for ever. The fishboat was beached and Mr. Abednego was handing up Johnny. Aunt Maury, bending low, took him up in her arms and staggered to her feet and with slow difficult steps carried him to a level spot and laid him down. Ellen was bleeding freely. She crawled on to the shingle and moved up nearer on hands and knees to watch, to help, to see what she had done, to stay humiliatingly outside any helping to repair what she had done.

Mr. Abednego then turned to her. His face was ugly with rage. He shouted at her. He cursed her. He roared, "You dom bitch, taking him out to drown him! Call yourself a woman! You haven't the brains of a louse! Hell, djever see a tide before, djever see that tide-rip coming round that there corner? You bloody fool that's what you are, a bloody daggit fool . . ."

Aunt Maury, who had laid Johnny on his stomach and drained what water she could out of him, turned for one moment and said loudly "HOLD YOUR TONGUE!" Her look fell on Ellen and on the blood which covered her face and stained her. She stopped working Johnny's arms for a second, pulled out her big handkerchief and threw it to Mr. Abednego with "Give her that". This he did, still growling.

"Served her right," he growled. "I seen it, the gun'le gouged her, mighta killed her, served her right, that tide, she mighta knowed, the blasted . . . "

Ellen heard the words pouring out, and, trying to stanch the place where she had been struck by something, she crawled on up the rocks toward the level place where Johnny lay. She did not dare to speak or disturb but watched his face and watched Aunt Maury who like God from Heaven worked his arms and pressed down on his body. Aunt Maury looked down at Ellen and in one motion ripped off her cotton shirt and threw it down the rock. "Help her, can't you?" she called to Abednego. He showed no disposition to help Ellen. He handed her the cotton shirt, muttering. He hated her and her stupidity, for the child's sake. He was indifferent to her blood and her distress.

The wordless knowledge flooded through Ellen that no life was possible to her now if this child died, not life with George nor any life, and as – looking upward – she crouched on the rock she was shot with the cruellest anguish that she must forgo this her life, for, if Nora's child did not live, she would go back into the sea. She could not look at Nora's face, nor Morgan's either.

She continued supporting herself on the sun-scented rocks and gazed up at Nora's inanimate child, shaking her vision free of blood, wiping it free. If he lived, she lived; if he was dead, she would fight her way past that angry old man if she had to, and she would plunge again at once into the current which – she gave a look – still raced strongly. She waited. She waited.

But Mr. Abednego was no longer between her and the sea. He had moved up and now stood silent apart from Mrs. Peake and the child, his hands on his hips, looking down at the boy. There was a terrible gravity in the scene, isolated from the summer day. Something within Mrs. Peake (who felt very much alone) said, If Dick were only here, if Dick were only here, but if Dick were here this would never have happened. If Dick were only here . . . and she worked steadily.

It was a long time before she sat back with the sweat pouring off her. A flutter had come to Johnny's face. His eyelids flickered and he raised a hand weakly as if to ward off, to expostulate. His shirt was torn off the shoulder where Ellen had grabbed it and for those saving moments in the press and suck of the water had caught his arm and held it fast.

Within the little boy a monstrous grievance awoke slowly and painfully. He began to whimper.

Thirty-Nine

WHEN THEY were back in the cottage and Johnny had drunk some milk and thrown it up again, and Ellen had tried to clean her face which had swollen and had started bleeding again, Aunt Maury made two great pads and had difficulty in contriving a bandage that would tie everything together; but she did it, after a fashion. In the meantime she had sent Mr. Abednego across to Mayne Island to tell Sturgeon to bring his speedboat immediately to take them all into Vancouver as quickly as possible. Ellen wanted to go with Mr. Abednego and telephone Nora at the Empress Hotel in Victoria telling her an easy version of what had happened, because – who knows – before the stern of the *Princess* had rounded the farther point and disappeared, some passenger might conceivably have seen the boat upset, and might or might not have seen the rescue, and that passenger might possibly tell Nora and terrify her, because her mind would at once fly to Johnny at that tip of land in the Pass. The thing seemed unlikely, and as time must not be wasted in getting Johnny home and as Ellen rapidly became a frightening object either wrapped or unwrapped and was not in very good condition, they took the chance of not telephoning. It was no good asking Mr. Abednego to do it. Aunt Maury could well imagine him – "That you, Mr. Peake . . . Senator . . . hay? Well, that blasted fool of a sister-in-law of yours tried to drown your boy in Active Pass today! Yeah, that's what I said. Yeah, tried to drown him. I told her . . . I said . . . " No, no, that would not do. They would have to take a chance – and against all likelihood the thing had happened. A friend of Morgan's standing at the ship's vanishing stern thought he saw a boat upset, no, he didn't know whether the occupants were drowned or not . . . bad place that Pass for drownings, but people . . . what? NO . . . ! You don't say so! At the tip of Active Pass? Yes . . . well, Morgan, I wouldn't for a million dollars . . . anyway there was another boat right there when I saw it . . . And Morgan was telephoning everywhere, and at Mayne Island he learned that Sturgeon's boat had gone to Mrs. Peake's place to take some people to Vancouver because there'd been an accident. No, they couldn't say for sure. Sawry, they couldn't say, it certny was too bad. So it was that when Aunt Maury telephoned Nora at once on arriving home, they had already left, and were flying back to Vancouver.

In clutching and holding Johnny Ellen had wrenched his arm badly and it was to be part of her punishment to see him in pain.

The doctor examined Johnny who now lay in his own white bed, and found nothing wrong that a day or two's quiet would not mend, except his arm. It was hard to tell how serious that might be until he could examine the boy properly. He then looked at Ellen's unrecognizable face. She would not go to the hospital as ordered, but waited to see Nora and Morgan. She prepared herself for hard treatment, deservedly. Above the storm of her feelings her face and head throbbed and ached. Aunt Maury with a few stains of blood on her skirt was there. Ellen did not load herself with self-accusations; in fact she spoke very little. Mr. Abednego who was the real saver of Johnny – and of Ellen – would perhaps, some day, sound splendidly funny. He had behaved true to form, which is often agreeable, and Aunt Maury tried to lift the whole thing to a prosaic level by making unfair fun of Mr. Abednego who had saved them. Ellen was grateful to him on every count including his being funny. Morgan would reward him materially, and better than that, he would make the journey to see Mr. Abednego who would frequently rehearse in years to come, "And the Senator he come all the way special from

Vancouver and wrang me by the hand . . . there was tears in his eyes . . . Mr. Abednego, he said to me, if ever a man . . . "
It was a pleasure to Ellen that he had cursed her thoroughly.

The telephone, ringing, announced a Mr. Harvey Pearce in Victoria. "I have been trying to get you. Morgan and Mrs. Peake caught the 4:30 plane. Is everything . . . ?"

"Yes, yes, I telephoned and heard that they'd left," said Aunt Maury. "Everything is all right."

Forty

THE PLANE flew no faster from Patricia Bay to Vancouver because two of the passengers were Mr. and Mrs. Morgan Peake who had suddenly learned that their son might be injured or dead. Morgan Peake and his wife sat side by side in the plane, and Nora, turning her head to the window to avoid communication and to indulge her fears alone, had the opportunity of seeing, this bright day, all those jewelled islands below, but she did not notice them. She remained silent, and her world, tumbling, was Johnny, and whether he still lived or no. The plane, for all its noise and sound, was killing her by standing still in the air (or so it seemed) and it was not until they landed on the Vancouver runway and Nora ran to the telephone, then ran and entered the taxi that had been ordered from Victoria, and the taxi sped on, that her tension became less unbearable. In the slow but evidently moving taxi, threading the traffic, they were making haste; in the swift plane they had stood still.

Vague intimations of responsibility for whatever had happened flickered in Morgan's mind and in the plane he spoke, at first, to his wife, who did not appear to hear him, so he said no more. He desired to console, to support her, but she seemed unaware of him. He put his hand over hers and she – isolated within, still with her head averted toward the window – took his hand, as a hand holds a piece of fabric, not as a hand holds a hand. She should not suffer so, she indulges herself, he thought rather impatiently, and he reiterated within himself that nothing might have happened – to Johnny at least. But there it was: she was consumed by anxiety for her only son: but Johnny was not Morgan's only son.

Sitting beside his wife in the plane, Morgan thought with relief, almost, of the other son, and how he went – unwillingly, and sat with his son – accepting, and then left – unwillingly, but saw each time that Gilbert was well cared for, and not actively unhappy; and he turned in thought almost for comfort to this vacant child, rather than think what might have befallen Johnny. And then he took himself to task again for being womanish and full of fear (because probably nothing had befallen Johnny) and he succeeded in thinking of Hartley and the Minister of Lands and Forests last night at dinner, and how it did some of these easterners good who had never been west before to learn a little about our northern potential in B.C., and he wished he could fly Hartley in to Kitimat, and beyond. Had they never seen a map, these fellows? And then he thought of Johnny again. He glanced at Nora who had turned from the window, but her eyes were closed. The plane was over Sea Island by this time, and this damned flight would soon be done.

Sitting in the plane then, and every minute since old Langley had said casually that there had been an accident in Active Pass and the accident had been traced to Aunt Maury's cottage, Nora had suffered extravagantly, beyond her power (she would have thought) to suffer; and so these two people had sat, in ignorance, side by side, together yet alone. Time, indifferent to them, passed in due course, and at last the taxi driver, slowing up excessively (the fool) to turn into the driveway, stopped at their door. Nora broke out of the taxi, into the house, and ran up the stairs.

Aunt Maury and Ellen were sitting in Ellen's bedroom near the room where Johnny was now asleep when the car drove up and Morgan and Nora came into the house. Ellen moved out of the room and stood with her hand on the banisters near Johnny's open door. They both came up the stairs, Nora running. She touched her sister as she passed – the bandaged face must have been some measure of what had happened.

She stood for a moment by the bed as if she were thinking Shall I wake him? Oh, I need to *feel* him, and Johnny stirred and woke and turned, and Nora bent, taking him in her arms, and Johnny cried out with the pain of his arm.

Morgan came up the stairs more heavily and as he looked at his sister-in-law some mask seemed gone away and there was a kind of tired unhappy dignity on his face. He put out his hand and patted her gently and said "Poor kid", and walked into the room. She went into her bedroom and nearly closed the door. She would tell them everything when they came out of Johnny's room.

"Shall I stay with you?" said Aunt Maury. She waited for a reply but Ellen did not seem to hear her, so she went out.

Soon Nora came into the room and her face was shining though the tears fell. She took both her sister's hands and kissed her on her sound cheek and looked at her.

Stumbling in her words, Ellen told them both the story, and turned away.

"Poor, poor Gypsy," Nora said, " . . . we are thankful and nothing, nothing else . . . it doesn't bear thinking of. Don't grieve so, please don't grieve, must she, Morgan? Tell her she mustn't grieve so!"

What magnanimity this was of Nora's, and of Morgan's too. There was never a word of censure. (How could you take him out in that tide! You know as well as anyone that you can't take a rowboat out in that rip-tide!) It seemed as if their closeness to great ultimate sorrow threw an illumination on the events that had so humbled Ellen, and enabled them to forgive. She could hardly refrain from tears in her abasement, so great was Nora's kindness, and Morgan's, when they might have met her harshly and with upbraiding. She longed to atone with humility – to take away from the past her frequent little scorns of the solid humourless Morgan who could treat her thus kindly when she had nearly drowned his son.

Aunt Maury told them, later, when they went downstairs, of Johnny's longing and hope deferred of seeing the seals, of his rushing to the cottage wailing, "Aunty says I can't go without my shirt, and I'll miss them! I'll miss them!"

The near-drowning of Johnny (and, of course, of Ellen) had implication beyond a danger, beyond a loss. It had to do with the attitude, or non-attitude, of Nora to Ellen and of Ellen's attitude to Nora which included her assumption that Nora by her adulation was doing things to Johnny which were clear to Ellen though not to her. And what had Ellen done, the smarty? With all her ways of the superior onlooker she had nearly drowned him, that's all. She had better mind her own business. Everyone had better mind their own business. A gap had closed.

A slightly ridiculous aspect of the whole affair – later – was that the near-drowning of the boy, and the near-hostility and reunion – which were important things – melted away, unless Ellen was able to keep a sense of proportion, before the visible wounds under her left eye. Simply because her face swelled and her narrowly escaped eye closed up and she had bandaged cuts which left ugly scars over the cheek-bone, she had to avoid being regarded as a heroine.

But now, waiting for something – she did not know what – she leaned heavily toward the window and looked on False Creek, and because she was sunk beneath relief and remorse and increasing pain and fatigue, she did not see the blue sky and water and a ship pushing through the water although her unbandaged eye rested on these things. (Beauty is intrinsic in the object alone, or in Ellen . . . or in someone else . . . ?) A cormorant, seated on the base of the statua, spread dark wings, but, for pleasure, Ellen might have been looking at Hogan's Alley.

There was telephoning and the arrangements were made. Aunt Maury had packed a little bag. "Come," said Morgan, taking hold of Ellen's arm, and Nora, walking quickly into the room, was very kind. By this time Ellen was not much aware of Morgan helping her down the stairs, and of Nora somewhere, and of Aunt Maury, still with blood on her skirt, sounding cheerful, and carrying the little bag to the car.

Forty-One

JOHNNY RAN into the room.

"Here's Aunty Gypsy back at last from the hospital," said Nora brightly.

Johnny stopped short and looked up at Ellen's cheek, scarred like a map. His blue eyes widened. He looked at her, moving his head this way and that way, scrutinizing, and forgot that his mother had said, "Now darling, when you see poor Aunty Gypsy don't stare at her and don't say anything at all about her face. She has some marks on it where the boat hit her, but the clever doctors are going to take them all away."

Johnny had said, "Yes, Mummy", but now, as he looked, blinking a little, repelled yet pleased by the large seam and the radiating puckers on his aunt's face, he forgot his mother's warning which in any case was nothing to remember compared to this exciting sight.

"Mummy," he said at last, and clearly, "Aunty Gypsy's ugly now, isn't she! What a pity!"

There was a silent formidable moment, and Johnny looked from face to face, surprised. The faces were changed and did not look lovingly at him. His mother spoke sharply in an unfamiliar voice.

"Don't ever say such a thing! I told you! How would you like it if someone said that to you!"

"You shouldn't pass remarks," said his father loudly, looking like thunder and promising thunder.

Johnny's world had in a moment become unpleasant just

because he had said that Aunt Gypsy was ugly; and so she was. He had never before been reproved sharply by his mother, there had been no need – or so it seemed – in all his years. His father was angry with him. Aunty Gypsy – bending toward him with a soft sound and then drawing back quickly – was queer. He looked again at these faces; his lower lip puckered; he opened his mouth and began to bawl. His mother bent quickly to him, still affronted, and led him, still bawling, from the room. Something familiar returned, and remained, as her arms went round him, but he preferred to continue bawling for the pleasure of it.

"When are you seeing those plastic fellows again?" asked Morgan, who was annoyed.

"Next week."

"They can do wonders. I knew a man . . . " But Morgan did not know a man. If it had been a broken leg, or ulcers, he would have followed the common course and said he knew a man . . . But he did not know a man whose face was badly scarred and then was made as good as new.

"A face to frighten the birds," said Ellen lightly. "I'm going upstairs to try on a hat, but they look grotesque. It's an experience, these hats, I assure you, Morgan. Good for one, probably." And she went. Johnny had been a test case.

That night Morgan paused beside his wife's dressing-table. "You've got to talk to that child about his Aunt Gypsy, or I will. He's got to realize that her face was knocked about because she saved him from drowning."

Nora, looking into her mirror, did not like Johnny to be called "that child".

She said coldly, "Everyone seems to forget that it was Gypsy who took him out there in the first place and nearly drowned him, and now everyone seems to think she's a heroine. I'm sorry for her, but she brought it on herself."

This was the first time that Nora had spoken slightingly of her sister. Many times she had put away, as a point of honour, her deep resentment of Gypsy's negligence in taking the child into danger. Nora had behaved remarkably well; she could bear shock or anxiety, but she could not tolerate Johnny being called "that child". It was monstrous that Morgan should call him "that child" in that tone.

"This is unworthy of you, Norrah," said her husband coldly, and went into the bathroom. In the separate rooms wife and husband pursued their lively annoyance. Then, "Well, good night," said Morgan, popping his head into the bedroom and back again as fast as possible.

"Oh, good night," said Nora, with her back to the bathroom door. When she got into bed she could not help seeing Gypsy's scarred face, and she felt sorry for her. The door opened, and Morgan in the dark said, "The price of casual negligence and danger often comes – ah – sometimes comes very high, disproportionately high, good night, dolling", and closed the door again.

Do we always live on a brink, then, said Nora to herself, lying there in the dark. Yes, I believe we do.

Mr. Hartley Pearce, member for North or was it South Indigo, who was an unknowing contributory cause of all this to-do, later made some unwise statements with reference to tariffs and foreign relations. These remarks were taken up by the Press and by the electors and, instead of becoming a Cabinet Minister in Ottawa, he lost his seat in the next election. It was, therefore, not necessary, after all, that Mr. and Mrs. Morgan Peake should have gone to Victoria and that Ellen should have been scarred on one side of her face for life; but who could tell.

Forty-Two

IF GEORGE and Ellen had lived together in happy marriage and had become as one, and if, then, an accident had occurred which had spoiled Ellen's undoubted beauty, the situation would have been different (she thought) from things as they were now. As it was, the dice were loaded against George.

She indulged in no self-pity, and would at any other time have regarded her disfigurement as the fair wages of folly and as a cheap price for Johnny's survival. This she would have accepted, and she would have gone her way as usual, chastened and only a little sorry. But now she could not bear it if George – not patient, rather tough, accustomed by nature and success to the best, selective – should marry her in the unwelcome rôle of impatient honourable man and should feel repugnance to her face and to living with her face by day and by night; nor could she bear it if George could not marry her because of her face. She took herself too seriously, no doubt.

Isa, always a few steps ahead in perception, wrote at once, "Don't agitate yourself about your face and George. Such things really don't matter, believe me. Hold your head high, scar and all, and if you have to think of yourself which for goodness sake don't, regard the whole thing as interesting but not serious."

All this may be true, but it does not alter the fact of George as a man committed and the left-hand side of my face, thought Ellen, avoiding any self-revelation to those around her who began to think with relief She does not care! What a good thing! Ellen saw in the bright light of her own dilemma the profound immemorial truth of old saws, born in the clash or slow rub of human experience – "It all depends whose ox is gored." My ox is untimely gored. Try it yourself, she thought, and see how you feel . . . but as for me, my ox is gored.

She wrote a long letter, speaking the truth as she saw it.

Forty-Three

GEORGE GORDON sat at his desk reading Ellen Cuppy's letter again. Then he put it in his inside pocket. He finished the day at his office, appointment after appointment, or conferences as his secretary preferred to call them, the theory being that a conference is more impressive than a talk, or an interview, or a meeting, or an appointment, and more is no doubt achieved by calling it a conference. He went home, then, from all these conferences to his flat, and after dinner he took the letter out and read it again. As a document it was honest, and repetitive. Ellen's honesty was hedged around by such limitations as "but you must see me while I'm ugly because they mightn't make a good job of it and then you wouldn't want to marry me after all", and "I'm not the placid kind, George, and I might be ten times harder to live with with this face, – it would make a difference in so many ways that we can't even think of", and "I'm trying to be wise enough and fair enough to stop this now, and not let you come. Because I could not bear compunction, or you coming and marrying me just to oblige", and "I would never feel you'd turned me down George", and "there, you're free".

Ellen was foolish enough not to transpose the situation and imagine George as having had an accident to his face and Ellen loving him more than ever with pride and tenderness, and marrying him. She was stupid not to think of this. George, however, did.

He took pen and paper and wrote:

"My dear Ellen, I love you. I told you this before many times and if because you have an accident to your face or your arm or your leg you think I don't love you any more, I could be angry with you. But I won't be because this is very tough, and I hope to God these plastic surgeons can make a good job – for you, not for me.

"Will you use a little imagination and think whether you'd want to leave me because I got bashed over the face. Well then don't be a little fool and get ideas. I shall arrive as planned on the Friday, and am coming by train as you suggest. I can't for the life of me see why – but if you say so. Dear Ellen.

Yours George – I love you."

George then went out and, under the street light, mailed his letter. Returning home, he entered the room in which were his desk and his books and a certain confusion which was cherished by him and respected by his housekeeper. The familiar room in the course of unpleasant time had come to be a cave in the hills, a retreat, and altogether his own. But tonight was a divisional point in time, and so the aspect of the room was not the same. It had already the estranged appearance of being no longer his own but subject to a future which included and was lighted by Ellen, scar or no. He accepted this willingly, indeed with impatience of delay, finding hardly anything to regret and everything to hope for. He packed, and left by the morning train with something like jubilation, in a new climate.

God help all dangerous ignorant young punks everywhere who sleep meditating mischief and wake – subhuman – to tedium and violence; but what about a congenital minx like George's once-wife Maidie who knows exactly what she is doing as she sits drumming her fingers and delicately meditating mischief.

She had become annoyed with Tom her husband, and was annoyed that she could no longer induce him to become annoyed. He seemed to have arrived at an impervious state of armed peace, and so, because her chosen weather was that of variable winds, provocation, connivance, talk, disclaimer, and because she had – at a distance – recently seen George Gordon looking vigorous and contented and younger than usual, she saw her way (she thought) to annoying Tom and – with luck – disturbing George. Her foot had until lately been on Tom's neck, but had somehow slipped.

She would telephone dear old George, strictly on business (" . . . surely there's no *law* against *that*, Tom!") She remembered, with the pleasant anticipation of a fencer, George's look of directness.

"George darling," she would say, "it's me. Just a matter of business. D'you remember those shares you got me ages ago . . . Algonquin Something or is it Algoma . . . well, I came across them and I don't *quite* understand . . . couldn't you come in and explain . . . " Anything would serve as long as it sounded like business. Tom would be annoyed and taken at a disadvantage, and George (she hoped) would be disturbed. She had not heard of Ellen Cuppy.

But when, in the evening, she telephoned in her light voice to George, he was not there.

"Mr. Gordon is out of town," said someone.

"Will he be back after the weekend?" How pleasant it was to be in touch with George again, or nearly in touch, even at this remove. She had probably been a fool ever to leave him for Tom.

"Mr. Gordon may be away some weeks . . . I don't know I'm sure . . . what might the name be?"

The name might be . . . no, Maidie considered, there was no name. She could turn, ingeniously enough, to some other direction for a diversion which she did not wish to postpone.

"No name," she said abruptly.

It was just as well, for her efforts would have been wasted. She and the past had lost their power to disturb George, who was now travelling westward. Whatever she might do, she could no more disturb him than could one of those thin pine trees in the dense forests through which he was passing, at that moment, on his way to Ellen; or shares in a common stock – once attractive – bought in the open market, then sold, and forgotten some time ago.

Forty-Four

EVERYBODY SEEMED to realize without being told that Ellen was in a state about going to the station to meet George Gordon, and conversations were held in her absence. The conversationalists usually said, "Such a mistake, not waiting until after the operation!"

At last, "If I came to the train with you to meet George, would it make it a bit easier," said Nora, "and we could take Johnny. He might divert . . . Children do . . . "

"No, Nora," said Ellen, looking at her sister and seeing the three of them – handsome Nora and Johnny and scarred Gypsy – walking like a deputation down the platform to meet George.

"My dear girl," said Aunt Maury the following day, "I'll come with you or not. As you like. It might help. Or perhaps you'd better go it alone. George doesn't need a civic welcome. As you like . . . "

"I think not, Aunt Maury," Ellen said, turning her soft right cheek toward Mrs. Peake as she so often seemed to do now. Not Aunt Maury, rolling sturdily beside her down the platform, a guardian, wearing such a hat; later, later, not now.

And then perversely she said to Morgan, so normal-formal, "Morgan, will you come with me to the station? No, don't have a meeting that night . . . put it off . . . or go late . . . but come with me and then go away. I'll drive us down and when George comes you can leave us and walk over to the Club or something."

Well really, thought Morgan, and said, "Of course, my dear Gypsy. I think I can come with you. It might be advisable. I mean to say I don't think it is necessary at all. I'll be glad, I mean . . ."

That night, Morgan said to his wife, "Dolling, I'm going with Gypsy to the station tomorrow night to meet this Gordon fellow." Well really, thought Nora. "I'll telephone you after from the Club."

Nora said, "Gypsy is a very strange person, but I suppose a thing like those scars *would* affect one. I still can't think why she didn't wait to see him till *after* the plastic business, not now", and she turned her fair face this way and that to the mirror, rubbing in the cream slowly, " . . . it is certainly too bad about her face, and of course we don't really know this George, what he is like . . . I hope, I'm sure, that it will be all right . . . "

Forty-Five

AFTER TRAVELLING far too long, the train pulled into the station at Vancouver and stopped. George was an experienced traveller but not marked by the dollar sign. He gave largesse and assembled his two bags and acquired the best red-cap smoothly and easily while other people bumbled about and met and talked and hovered pointing over the baggage.

The railway station, as in most cities, was dim, and although there were lights, the lights were refracted and split so that one did not identify people clearly, what with lights and shadows and the hurrying and meeting and passing and repassing of passengers who all got off the train because this was a terminal station.

George arrived by train rather than by air in order to oblige Ellen. This seemed silly to him, but he supposed she had some reason for the request – or, rather, order; and he was to learn in many future years that there was usually good reason behind the funny things she said or did, and so he learned to trust her almost as well as he loved her, but not quite.

A landing at an airport is an unequivocal business. In comes this highly specialized machine. It decants its passengers in flat daylight or nightlight upon the flat and open runway which is part of the flat and open plain. They move hastily, charging forward all together, as if, by association, the margin of time were still small, into the well-lighted and unpleasant waiting-room where people are always waiting, loitering, often with a mechanized watching look which they catch – in part – from their surroundings. A little unsuitable plush might help; or rose candle shades laden with dust might humanize. This was no kind of a place for Ellen to meet her lover again, and she knew it; and that was the reason why George, looking over the heads and between the heads of men and women with hats on, saw Ellen afar down the railway station platform, walking with her light careless step beside a heavily-built double-breasted man, a man who walks like a bear, no doubt Morgan Peake, M.P. Ellen was taller than this man by almost half her bare head. She held her head well, regardless, and the slanting and broken lights showed Ellen, but not what she looked like.

George, having seen them, walked quickly toward them, pushing between people. He took her in his arms almost before he spoke. He kissed her cheek, and the shiny and seamed and puckered skin was repellent to him. Then he kissed her well, out of love and pity and delight. He took her arm and they turned. Ellen walked beside him. Suddenly she snatched her arm away and whirled round.

"George, this is Morgan!" she exclaimed, but Morgan did not seem to be there. It was of no consequence. They resumed walking very slowly, and this was the actual beginning of their happy chequered life together.

Afterword

BY ANNE MARRIOTT

The title of this, Ethel Wilson's last published novel, implies the whole of its plot. Love and salt water – they are the antagonists who dominate the story, powerful forces which will be in combat to the death before the book ends. The course of one (in its varied forms) will be forever altered by the other.

In a lecture Wilson gave at the University of British Columbia in 1957, she described how *Love and Salt Water* had its genesis. Already she had written, with intense observation and feeling, about the "Upper Country," the interior of British Columbia, notably in *Swamp Angel* which had been published in 1954. But after that she felt that she must, for what she called her "own peace," write a novel about the coast region, its people, its breakers and inlets and shores.

One day, in Vancouver's Stanley Park, which lies by and is in a close relationship with the sea, Wilson saw, she told her University of British Columbia audience, three people out for a walk. Apparently father, mother, and beautiful young daughter, they appeared to be the epitome of well-being – happy, healthy, and prosperous. They looked, Wilson said, to be people to whom nothing untoward could ever happen.

But Wilson knew that in the best-planned lives "dreadful private casualties" could occur. What might those be in the future of that golden trio? The three, whose identity she never knew, and whom she never saw again, took over her novelist's imagination. They became the Cuppys – Mr., Mrs., and

Ellen – and as Wilson established their characters, the coastal book she envisioned began to grow.

The daughter, Ellen, was to be the heroine of the novel. In fact, the story's first title was *Miss Cuppy*. Wilson began to write it in the first person, but returned to her favourite literary device, the omniscient narrator who, in addition to knowing what goes on in all the characters' minds, can interject comments, philosophical or otherwise, whenever she/he wishes.

At the beginning of the story, we become aware that the Cuppy household is pervaded by love. Nora, Ellen's older sister, is about to marry a devoted suitor. Ellen and her mother are dear companions. Mr. Cuppy's husbandly, fatherly affection embraces them all. Salt water, a fringe of the vast Pacific, stretches calm and reflective in the sheltered reaches of English Bay and Vancouver harbour near their home. Watched by the Cuppys, craft of all kinds move on this peaceful sea, observed also by myriads of seabirds, including the dusky cormorants. Do the cormorants hint at something dark, mysterious? Suddenly, the first dreadful casualty strikes: Mrs. Cuppy dies.

Soon after this early point in the novel, we recognize another of Wilson's preferred literary contrivances – the journey. Her characters move to and fro like the coming and going of the tides. She establishes in the second chapter a sense of the constant shifting of existence by emphasizing the continuous passage of freighters in and out of the Vancouver roadstead.

"Some day, when Father has time . . . we'll go on a freighter," Mrs. Cuppy had promised Ellen. But Ellen and her father have to go on their own, the voyage a remedy for their grief over Mrs. Cuppy's death.

Wilson uses this voyage as setting for the first great battle between the two antagonists, salt water and love. On the Atlantic, a strange ocean to the west-coasters, she creates a violent storm, significantly at Christmas, festival of love. (Wilson is at her best as a writer when she describes storms. One of her most disturbing, memorable short stories is another duel between love and salt water, "From Flores," in the collection *Mrs. Golightly and Other Stories*.) The scene in which the raging sea bursts open the porthole of Ellen's snug cabin and the water rushes in shocks the reader with its symbolism.

Another foreshadowing of the novel's course takes place when the young member of the freighter's crew who calls himself a "sea-boy" is swept away and drowned. Love, however, is not without its victories, as the father, Frank Cuppy, finds new life and consolation in a fellow-passenger in spite of, or perhaps because of, the storm.

Ellen's engagement and its breaking seem only an interlude in the story. A new journey takes her to Saskatoon, to live, to work, and eventually to be wooed by George Gordon, safely out of reach of the unpredictable sea. But salt water has not finished with Ellen yet – we sense that it never will.

Wilson transfers Ellen back to Vancouver for a visit. There the girl takes charge of Johnny, the adored child of her sister Nora. It is now mother-love, or substitute-mother-love, that is pitted against salt water.

It is a little hard to believe that Nora, besotted by her child, would allow Ellen to take him to an aunt's cottage on Galiano Island, close by Active Pass, a famous danger spot on the British Columbia coast. Hard to believe, even if Nora leaves Johnny to further her husband's political career. Harder still to credit that Ellen, an experienced coast-dweller, would forget about the rip tide in the Pass, not to mention the steamer which passes through it daily between Vancouver and Vancouver Island. But life, Wilson declared, sets traps for all, into which all of us fall. Life sets such a trap for Ellen, who, in her desire to fulfil Johnny's longing to look for seals, takes him out into the Pass in a small rowboat.

Johnny is compared in looks to a cherub. Remembering the "sea-boy" who looked like a Botticelli angel, we are alarmed. We know disaster is about to overtake this child. The tide rips through the Pass. The huge wave from the steamer's wake combines with the rip to upset the rowboat. Johnny and Ellen struggle in the wild salt water. (Mr. Abednego, the fisherman who rescues them, is one of the exactly drawn, instantly recognizable minor characters who are a delight in all Wilson's books.)

The images evoked by the novel's title permeate its characters as well as its action. Aunt Maury, owner of the Galiano Island cottage, who works desperately to revive the unconscious Johnny, bears the marks of both love and salt water, but in her they are complementary rather than opposed. Salt water runs in her veins, we are told, but she is also a beneficent ship, a rescue vessel with "a fine plain face like a ship's figurehead."

Will love or salt water be the winner in the climactic contest? Ethel Wilson herself was not sure. She wrote two endings to the novel, one the published version in which Johnny is restored, the other in which he dies. Worried that the "happy ending" might be considered banal, Wilson sent the second conclusion to John Gray, her friend and editor at the Macmillan Company, for his opinion. Shorter than the one familiar to us, this alternative ending has Aunt Maury and Mr. Abednego bearing the small lifeless body of the child up to the island cottage, while Ellen, distraught with remorse, plunges back into Active Pass. Her body is never recovered. But the "happy ending" was selected. Love prevails.

In any analysis of a novel, it is interesting to perceive how the writer has transmuted the pervasive events of his or her life into the fiction. This process is apparent in Ethel Wilson's books, in particular her use of the journeying theme, as even a quick scanning of her biography will prove. Lesser occurrences are also utilized – in *Love and Salt Water* a broken engagement and subsequent feelings of guilt.

Studying her life, one sees that love, as evidenced in her long, happy marriage, was arbiter of much of Wilson's existence. But salt water influenced it greatly, both in her living and her writing, literally and figuratively. In all of literature, the ocean has been a simile for change, sorrow, and death, and they were grim waters of disease and suffering that overwhelmed Wilson in her last years. But she held a determined faith that this life was not all, there was more to come. In the end, love would triumph, would be the victor of the two antagonists.

Love and Salt Water is the slightest of Wilson's novels (her own word for it was "temperate"), in spite of the momentous subjects with which it deals. One of these, of course, is mental handicap, and the treatment of Gilbert reveals how attitudes have changed since Wilson was writing. But because of the slightness of plot, the novel offers a special joy. Not, perhaps, deeply involved with the story, the reader is left free to revel in Wilson's elegant writing style, her exact choice of words, her economy, clarity – luminosity, even. "Small nameless ducks her in procession on the outgoing tide . . . with their wake of following glitter." The writing stands out like embroidery on the paler stuff of the tale, or to look to salt water for metaphor, the writing is like the bright patterns of foam which enliven the duller surface of the ocean.

BY ETHEL WILSON

FICTION
Hetty Dorval (1947)
The Innocent Traveller (1949)
The Equations of Love (1952)
Swamp Angel (1954)
Love and Salt Water (1956)
Mrs. Golightly and Other Stories (1961)

SELECTED WRITINGS
Ethel Wilson: Stories, Essays, and Letters
[ed. David Stouck] (1987)